OVER KILL

A DCI SEAN BRACKEN NOVEL

JOHN CARSON

DCI SEAN BRACKEN SERIES

CALVIN STEWART SERIES

Final Warning

DI FRANK MILLER SERIES

Crash Point

Silent Marker

Rain Town

Watch Me Bleed

Broken Wheels

Sudden Death

Under the Knife

Trial and Error

Warning Sign

Cut Throat

Blood from a Stone

Time of Death

Frank Miller Crime Series – Books 1-3 – Box set

Frank Miller Crime Series - Books 4-6 - Box set

MAX DOYLE SERIES

SCOTT MARSHALL SERIES

Old Habits

OVER KILL

For my writing buddies again. Bear and Bella

ONE

Twenty years ago

If they had gone to the other shopping centre like he wanted, nobody would have died.

But they didn't, and Ray Chisolm's wife would die almost a week later, in a dimly lit close off the High Street.

'Some manky chicken that's been squeezed into a round shape, or beef that like looks anything but?' He stood at the deli counter dramatically stroking his chin.

'Come on, for God's sake, the lassie's waiting,' Diane said, nudging him in the ribs.

'What do you think, Carly?' he said to his oldest daughter. At three and a half, she just giggled.

'You choose,' she said to him.

He turned round to look at his newborn daughter, who was in her car seat sitting in a high trolley behind him. 'What do you think...' he started to say and stopped dead. There was a man holding the baby's arm, pumping it up and down.

'Hello, darlin',' the clarty bastard was saying to her.

'Hey. What the fuck are you on?' Ray said.

The man had a look about him that was almost at tramp level. Scruffy clothes, unkempt hair, unshaven, wild eyes.

'What's your fucking problem?' the man answered.

Ray immediately went on the defensive. 'Leave my daughter alone,' he said, just waiting for the man to let his daughter's arm go so he could get her safely out of the way. The man did so, and Diane quickly moved the trolley aside.

'My problem is, that's my daughter. Keep your filthy fucking mitts off her.'

'Or else what?'

'Or else you'll find out,' Ray said, taking a step forward, but he felt a hand on his arm.

'Forget him, Ray,' Diane said.

Ray looked the other man in the eyes before turning to his wife. 'You're right. I just don't know where the dirty bastard's hands have been.'

They walked away, Diane pushing the trolley now, Carly helping her. Ray walked behind them and they turned into an aisle.

'My hands are clean!' the tramp screamed at the top of his voice.

That would have been the end of it for Ray if the man had walked away, but he didn't let it go. He followed them into the aisle.

'My fucking hands are clean!' he shouted again.

'Why don't you piss off, fucking pervert?' Ray said as Diane walked away from the man.

'Don't you call me a pervert!' the man screamed. He was fast. Ray made a mistake that could have been a fatal one: he turned his back on the man.

It was an opening the tramp took advantage of. He threw himself at Ray, grabbing him and slamming him against the shelves. It only took Ray a second to recover from the attack. He pushed the tramp back, and the tramp brought both hands round in an arc, obviously trying to smack them against Ray's ears, but Ray's reflexes were quick and he tilted his head back and the tramp's hands missed.

Ray had been in a few fights, mostly when he was drunk and his reflexes were slower, but he was sober now and they were so much faster. A surge of adren-aline rushed through him and he pushed the tramp back, raging now. He threw the tramp onto cartons of orange juice and held him there.

'Go on then, big man!' the tramp shouted at him. 'Go on then!'

Ray was about to punch the man in the face, but he didn't. It was almost as if he was in a trance at that point; he didn't remember exactly when his fingers found the tramp's throat, but he would remember his fingers being sore to fully open for days afterwards. Right at that moment in time, though, they were clamped firmly around the tramp's throat. And he was squeezing like his life depended on it.

There was a black haze around him. Nothing else existed in that moment. It was just him pinning down the tramp, looking into his eyes. He wasn't aware of any other sound.

Wasn't aware of the men who were rushing at him. Until they grabbed his arms and hauled him back, slamming him into the shelves on the other side, just where the tramp had shoved him. Four men stood there looking at him as the tramp got up and started running in the opposite direction.

'Get your fucking hands off me,' Ray said, pulling his arms free. He saw that one man was wearing a security guard's uniform, two were wearing white shirts – obviously employees – and one was wearing civilian clothing.

'I've called the police,' the older white-shirted man said.

'Who the fuck are you?' Ray spat.

'I'm the store manager. You're going to get arrested.'

'Do you mind stopping swearing, sir?' the plain-clothed man said.

Ray looked at him. 'Who the fuck are you?'

'Store detective,' he said. 'You're scaring other customers.'

'Me? What about that arsehole?'

'You're getting arrested for attacking that man,' the manager said.

'Really now? Check your CCTV. He touched my baby, followed us round here and then attacked me. I was defending myself when you grabbed me.'

There was a visible change in the manager's face, that *'oh, shit'* moment when the penny dropped and he could see his pension flying away along with the tramp.

'Christ. Get on to mall security and get him stopped!' he barked at the store detective. 'Now! Don't let him get away.'

The four men rushed away and Ray walked up to the end of the aisle, where his wife and kids were waiting.

A little while later, he looked and saw a uniformed

police officer walking towards him, directed by store security.

'Tell me what happened,' the man said.

Ray went through all the details, and then a voice crackled through the officer's handset and he spoke into his radio.

'They got him trying to board a bus,' he explained.

'The bastard's not that daft after all,' Ray said.

'That's the thing: he was released from Gogarburn psychiatric hospital a few weeks ago. Care in the community. The procurator fiscal won't touch him. Sorry, sir. I understand your frustration, but that's the way it works.'

Ray nodded and bit back the remarks he had swimming inside his head. He was glad he wasn't getting arrested.

'I'm so sorry about the mix-up,' the manager said, handing Diane a bouquet of flowers.

'I don't know why they released all those people when they're obviously not right,' she said.

The manager smiled at her. 'I'm so sorry,' he said again, and walked away.

'What's going to happen the next time he grabs a child?' she said to Ray. 'Maybe the next time he'll get away with it, snatching a kid.'

'Bastard. He's damn lucky. I would have gone away for a long time if I'd killed him.'

'Life's not fair, Ray. This justice system is flawed beyond belief.'

'You're telling me. But next time I don't care: if he comes near any of us again, there'll be a very different outcome.'

Diane let Carly carry the flowers.

TWO

For the second time that week, PC Eddie McGowan was giving the patrol car a bloody good hiding, just so he could get back to the station and his poker game.

'Easy there! Christ. I nearly put my coffee about myself,' Sergeant Stan Morrison said to his partner. It had been a while since he had been partnered with the younger officer, and it was either come out for this night shift or hang himself. It could have gone either way as he was standing in front of the bathroom mirror, with the shift winning out at the end of the day as he clipped his tie on.

'Join the polis, they said. It'll be fun, they said,' McGowan growled as the headlights cut through the darkness of the country road.

'What are you havering about now?' Morrison said, giving up on trying to sip the hot liquid through the little hole in the lid. Maybe he should just throw it about the moaning bastard, give him something to really whine about. Maybe it would make him think twice about complaining all the time if he had to rub Sudocrem into his bollocks every night for a week.

'This place we're going to. My heebies are being jeebied as we speak.'

'What the fuck does that mean? You been watching *Star Wars* again?'

'This place. The nuthouse. I got the heebie-jeebies when we got the call.'

Morrison shook his head as the patrol car's headlights cut a swathe through the darkness.

'First of all, it hasn't been a nuthouse, as you so eloquently put it, for a very long time. And second, it's a manky old building that YouTubers and explorers go into regularly, even though they're not supposed to. So man up and stop acting like a wee lassie. You're polis, you carry a weapon. You're supposed to meet anything head on.'

'Shite. I hate this job. I only took it because there was nothing else. My wife said it would be a good career move. What does she know? She thought it was a good career move when they promoted her in Tesco from the bakery to the deli.'

'Did you hear the one about the guy getting fired for putting his nob in the meat slicer?' Morrison said.

'Naw.'

'He got fired. And the meat slicer got fired as well.' He looked at McGowan for a second. 'Your wife's no' the meat slicer, is she?'

'She cuts everything. Meat, cheese.' He knitted his eyebrows. 'Fuck knows what else there is to cut.'

Morrison rolled his eyes. This was going to be a fun shift, but if that bastard thought he was going to rush through every job just so he could get back to his cards, he could go whistle.

'It's a vandal call, that's all. Probably some wee ponce going about with a camera, filming some crap to upload.'

'Or it could be haunted.' McGowan was gripping the wheel like he wanted to rip it off and eat it.

'What? Haunted? Are you daft? It's an old building they're going to turn into flats. And slow it down a bit, ya hoor. It's a quiet night, so we can draw this one out a bit if you'd stop driving like you're touching cloth.'

McGowan relaxed a bit as he drove the car along the country road towards the abandoned asylum. He hadn't thought it would be this hard working in St Andrews, but apparently somebody had other ideas for him. He shook his head, thinking about how he would word his resignation. Maybe start with something simple like, *You can shove your job up your jacksie.*

Superintendent Keith was a ginger radge, and McGowan could see the older man's face now, reddening like he was about to let one rip, but McGowan would be beyond caring at that point. He was picturing burning his uniform when a shout brought him back to the here and now.

'Watch! Fence!' Morrison shouted.

'What?' McGowan said, taking his eyes off the road for a moment, just long enough for the fence securing the property to sneak up on them and throw itself at the front of their car. Or at least that's how McGowan felt it went down.

The fence crashed against the bodywork of the patrol car and McGowan, eyes now front, slammed the brakes on as the battle of the metals screeched all around them. The front tyres did their bit in trying to stop them in time but sticks of liquorice wrapped round the wheels would have been just as effective.

Morrison gave up any hope of finishing his coffee as momentum grabbed it and threw it at the inside of the windscreen.

'Jesus, did you not see that fucking fence?' he yelled at McGowan.

'Oh aye, I saw it and thought, fuck it, I'll just drive over the top o' it.'

Morrison briefly wondered if that had really been the case and McGowan was being flippant. 'You could have killed us. Lucky it was just my coffee and not my heid that skelped that windscreen.'

McGowan ignored him and got out to see what the damage was. Morrison wondered if the younger man was thinking about what literary flair he could add to the report about how they were driving one minute and playing dodgem cars the next.

The fence was around the property, which would stop cars getting close to the old hospital, but a hungry YouTuber with a will and a camera would find his way in.

'You want me to call it in?' McGowan said.

'Call it in? And tell them what? We couldn't find the entrance so you decided to create your own?' Morrison shook his head. 'Aye, call it in after we're done looking.'

'You did say you wanted us to string this one out.'

'Aw, shut up, halfwit. You're lucky one of us didn't break our bloody neck. Let's go and check this out, and by Christ, we better no' catch some wee scally bastard in there or I'll shove his camera up his arse.'

McGowan stood and looked at the old building, which was like some ghostly mansion in a horror film. During the day, the building was red stone with ornate exterior features. At this time of night, it was a grey shadow, the windows hiding secrets behind them.

A cold wind rattled the branches of the trees that surrounded the property.

'Just call it in and tell them we didn't see anything,' McGowan said, shivering.

'Don't talk pish. Wee lassie.'

Morrison walked forward, his torchlight sweeping around the grounds, chasing the shadows from the depths of the nooks and crannies.

'Look. Over there,' he said, and McGowan followed the path of the light and caught sight of the board that had been pulled loose at the front door.

'Maybe you could start your own YouTube channel. Call it something like, *Big Fanny Explores Scotland.*'

'Bloody hilarious. I'd make a lot more money doing that than I would this.'

They climbed the stone steps leading up to the entrance.

'I wonder what this place was, back in the day?' McGowan asked. 'Before it housed the psychiatric patients, like.'

'It belonged to a rich family years ago, before they sold it. Then it was turned into an asylum.'

'Let's just get in and tell them there was nae stooshie and then get the hell out.'

Morrison rolled his eyes. He just hoped the

younger man would have his back if an axe-wielding maniac jumped out.

They went in through the gap in the boards at the front door, Morrison having to suck his gut in a little bit more than McGowan.

They shone their torches around, the light bouncing off the grand staircase straight in front of them. Paint was flaking off the walls like dying flesh. The stone floor in the entrance was littered with old plaster that had either fallen off the walls or been helped on its way.

But it wasn't this that caught the policemen's attention. It was the wheelchair sitting in the middle of the room. Or rather the photograph that sat on it.

Morrison walked over to it, his torchlight held off to one side so the bright light wouldn't reflect off the shiny photo paper. He studied the image for a moment before turning to look at McGowan.

'Looks like it's going to be a busy night after all.'

THREE

'Where does Chaz think you are tonight?' Catherine Bracken asked her ex-husband.

'I don't see her every night. She does things in her spare time too,' Detective Chief Inspector Sean Bracken said.

'That's not what I asked.'

She smiled at him as they walked along the Shore in Leith. The night air was cold, fireworks flying through the air thanks to irresponsible little bastards trying their hardest to maim each other and cause general mayhem. Setting fires would come later, when they had run out of firewood to put on their bonfires.

'I might have mentioned it,' he replied with what he hoped was his best *lying bastard* face.

'No, you haven't. You have your *lying bastard* face on.'

He had practised that face for years, sometimes in the mirror, a face he thought he had perfected and was known only to him. But he might have guessed he couldn't pull the wool over Catherine's eyes.

'Let me finish. I was saying I might have, but probably haven't.'

'What are you like? You could have told her that I asked you out for a drink because I want to talk to you about something.'

'I could have. I could have also tried a homemade colonic-irrigation kit with a garden hose, but I didn't do that either.'

He held the door open for her at the Ship on the Shore pub and they stepped into the warmth, leaving behind the shriek of rockets and tinny explosions.

Catherine smiled and waved at a woman sitting on her own. The woman, who looked to be around forty or knocking on the door, smiled and waved back. Catherine led the way into battle, squeezing past regulars who were in the pub supporting a local cause. Bracken thought it might have been 'sponsor your local landlord' night by the way they were scooping back the pints.

'Usual?' he asked Catherine.

'I might have a new usual now, Sean,' she said, smiling at him.

'Then it would still be your usual.'

'*Touché*. G and T, please.'

'After that wee dance, we circle back to the fact that your usual is still gin,' he said, making a face that a disapproving headmaster might give to the brightest girl in school after she just set fire to it.

Catherine laughed. 'I like pulling your chain.'

'Don't be saying that too loudly in front of Leon,' he answered, then gave the barman his order. 'Can you see if there's a free table? Preferably not with that woman.'

'She's nice. She works with me.' Catherine turned away and managed to find a table tucked away in the corner.

Bracken followed with his pint and the smaller glass. 'Seems a bit of a busy place for a woman to be drinking on her own,' he said, putting the glasses down.

'It's not like she's going to be shanghaied, Sean. She was meeting a new boyfriend in here.' She looked past the crowd of men and saw the woman was still sitting on her own.

'Jack the Ripper have a wee swally in here, does he?' Bracken said, sipping his pint. He wanted to look past the other drinkers at the woman, but that might give the wrong impression.

'She met him online. He seems a nice bloke. A lot younger than her, but they hit it off.' She clinked his glass. 'Cheers.'

'Cheers –' *love* he was about to say, like in the old days, but caught himself in time.

Catherine figured out his verbal blunder and had the good grace to ignore it. Well, except for giving him a smile that let him know she knew.

'Right then, you wanted to have a wee chat with me tonight,' he said, feeling a beamer touch his cheeks. *It's just the heat in the place,* he told himself. *You came in here from the cold and now the warmth of the place is making you hot. Nothing to see here – move along, folks.*

'Getting right down to business,' Catherine said. 'I wonder if the girls who frequented this place a hundred years ago got right down to business?'

'Don't say that too loudly. They might think that's what we're doing. I have a reputation to think about.'

She laughed. 'Too late for that. But you're right. This isn't a social evening. I want your advice on something.'

Bracken sipped his pint, trying to read Catherine's face, but he obviously wasn't as good at it as she was. 'Go on then, I'm all ears.'

'It's Leon.'

'I knew it. What did you find out? He's been catfishing you all this time?'

'Listen, will you? He's talking about getting married.'

'To you?'

'Well, you'd have something to worry about if it was Sarah. Yes, me.' Sarah was their twenty-two year old daughter.

'Right. And you're having doubts.'

'Not so much doubts. I'm on the fence. I mean, he's nice enough –'

'But he's all whistle and no kettle.'

'Is that a euphemism for not being able to get it up?' she asked.

'What? Of course not. How long you been seeing him now?'

'Three months or so.'

'Plenty of time to know whether you like the man or not.'

'I haven't slept with him.' Catherine took a sip of her drink and looked down at the table for a moment, not able to meet her ex-husband's eyes. When she eventually looked up, he was swirling his pint, looking into the white head for inspiration.

Then he looked back at her.

'That says a lot about a relationship,' he said in a quiet voice. 'You mind if I ask why?'

She shook her head. 'I wouldn't have mentioned it if I minded. The thing is...How can I put this without sounding like a real bitch? I don't fancy him.'

Bracken made a surprised face. 'You've been going with him for three months and you couldn't tell before he started writing his own wedding vows that there wasn't an attraction there? Or do you just bag off with him in the dark?'

'Bloody hell, Bracken, *bag off*? I haven't done that since high school. Bag off. Now you make me feel like a sixteen-year-old.'

'You know what I mean. If you have a fumble in the dark and he's thinking he's getting his leg over, how does he take it when you reject him?'

She shrugged. 'He tells me he loves me and that he can wait.'

'There's clearly something wrong with him. I mean, we didn't wait three months.'

Catherine looked at him for a moment, as if reliving their first time together in her head. 'You took me out for a fish supper one night, then nailed me on your couch.'

'Hey, that was a good fish supper. I didn't hear you complain. I even bought you a bottle of Irn-Bru.'

'Yeah, you must have guessed you would be getting lucky that night,' she said.

'Social convention dictated that since that was the third date, I had an obligation to pursue a means to our mutual satisfaction that night.'

'Only you achieved satisfaction, since you were flying solo.'

'You make it sound like you weren't even in the

room.'

'You know what I mean.'

'Listen, the fish supper filled me up. It zapped my energy. If I could have gone on, I would have, but what with the food and me getting up early the next day –'

Catherine smiled and put a hand on his. 'Don't worry, you made up for it later on. But my point is, we fooled around, I fell in love with you and I couldn't wait to get married to you. But it's different with Leon. I don't want to get married to him. It's too soon.'

'You can't marry him unless you're a hundred per cent sure,' Bracken said, and something booted him in the guts. A feeling sat there, like when he had run for a bus one day and the bastard had pulled away and he was left with a stitch.

'I know that. Leon was a good laugh at first, and he still is, but I just can't make the next move with him. I don't know what it is.'

Bracken was going to come out with a quip like, *When you've had steak, it's hard to settle for hamburger,* but he bit his tongue.

'I'm no expert, but I think you have to feel something inside for a person you've been dating. It's not like going to a singles' club and hooking up with somebody, and you both know you're going to have fun and then go your separate ways in the morning. This is different.'

'You're right. I met him online and we hit it off, but something's not right.' She took a drink. 'I think being the ex-wife of a copper has made me overly suspicious.'

'There's no such thing as overly suspicious. You have a gut feeling, that's all.' Bracken sipped his pint. 'You want me to run him through the system?'

'You've already done that. I can tell. You have another one of your faces on. The one where you try to look all innocent, but your lips go all funny.'

'Look, it was only because Sarah still lives at home. I'm not denying I did it, obviously. His name didn't pull up any red flags.'

Catherine smiled again. 'I don't blame you, but I do want to know if you found anything out.'

Bracken shook his head. 'There're no skeletons in the closet.'

'My friends did tell me that I should proceed with caution when I told them about Leon. They said he would turn out to be an axe murderer or something.'

'Is that why you wouldn't sleep with him? You thought there was maybe something in his past that you didn't know about? Everybody has a past, Cath.'

'I know, but there's the trust issue.'

Bracken looked at her, knowing full well about trust issues in a marriage. Catherine had cheated on him after all.

'Anyway, thanks for listening. I just wanted to vent.'

'That's what I'm here for.'

'Let me ask you: do you think you and Chaz are heading for the altar?'

'I'm not sure. I'm just taking everything one day at a time.'

'Let's get another drink. All I've got to go home to is an empty flat.'

'At least you have a flat. My offer on a flat was beaten again.'

'You've got the guest house to go home to. Your dad. His dog, Max. Bob and Mary.'

'Do you miss going out with them as a foursome?' Bracken asked, standing up to get another round in.

Catherine didn't hesitate. 'Yes, I do. I miss our Saturday nights out.'

Bracken went to the bar and got more drinks in. He wondered what Leon's real intentions were. Did he want to use her? If so, why had he stuck around for three months without sleeping with her?

He took the drinks and sat back down. They chatted just like old times and had a laugh. Bracken felt guilty for a moment, being out with another woman and not telling Chaz, but it wasn't like he was cheating on his girlfriend.

After a couple of hours, they left the warmth of the

pub and went out into the cold night. The war zone that was Guy Fawkes Night continued unabated. Fireworks above reflected off the river as they walked along the Shore, past the King's Wark pub.

'This city seems to never sleep these days,' Bracken said.

'It's growing. It's called progression, but I don't think Ed would see it that way.'

'No, I don't think my dad would see it like that. Too many people, too many cars, he would say. Not enough German shepherds, though.'

'He does tend to like dogs more than people.'

'I don't entirely blame him.'

They walked up Sandport Place and stopped at the entrance to her stairway.

'Coming up for a drink?'

Bracken hesitated, looked at his watch and blew his breath into the cold night air. 'I really should be getting up the road.'

'One for the road?'

He was on the fence now. Then he thought about what was waiting for him up the road: his own wee room in the guest house. Netflix on his iPad if nobody was in the guest lounge.

'Aye, go on then.'

They walked in and took the lift to Catherine's apartment.

FOUR

'Sit!' Ed Bracken held up the tennis ball as his dog stood looking expectantly at him. 'Come on, for God's sake. You've done this before.'

Max barked.

'Did I say shout in the house? Did I? Indeed I did not. Now, sit!'

The German shepherd stood looking at him and barked again.

'What's wrong with your heid? You know how to sit.' Ed showed the big dog his tennis ball again.

Bob Long, retired detective inspector and owner of the guest house, walked into the lounge.

'Max! Sit!' he said, taking a dog biscuit out of his pocket. The dog sat and Bob gave him the treat.

'Aw, what's that all about?' Ed complained.

'Psychology, pal. He knows he'll get his tennis ball

off you later on when you take him for a walk. That's a given. Right now, though, I have the treat, so he wants that more than he wants a manky ball.'

'Maybe I'll train Bob with those treats,' Mary, Bob's wife, said as she came into the lounge. Max wagged his tail, stood up, went over to her and rubbed himself against her legs.

'Listen, it's going to take a lot more than dog treats to make me do as I'm told,' Bob said.

Ed shook his head. 'No need to put a brave face on it for me, son.'

Mary made a face and shook her head. 'He's dreaming, Ed. You should see him with his apron on through the back.' She giggled and left the room.

'Aye, right. Just you wait,' Bob said when she was out of the room. He turned to look at Ed. 'You don't think she heard me, do you?'

'I hope she did. That would serve you bloody right.'

'What's with all this training Max?' Bob asked, eager to steer the conversation away from the possibility of getting his balls in a vice.

'I'm going out on a date this afternoon with my new lady friend, Elizabeth. Or, as my uncouth son says, that floozy. I thought about bringing her back here for a cup of tea, if that's alright with you? Before she goes to the hotel.'

'Of course it is.'

'I thought I would show her how well trained Max is. But look at him. I could train a bloody log of wood better.'

'Why does she need to see him doing tricks?' Bob said.

'It's not just tricks, Bob. It's commands. I might have given Elizabeth the impression that Max is super-intelligent. Just to impress her.'

'And now what? You've got six hours to turn him into a police dog? Maybe you should have gone for describing him as a big softie.'

'Patience. He'll get there.' Ed looked at the dog. 'Sit!'

Max stood looking at him.

'Stand!'

Max kept standing.

'Good boy!' Ed tossed the dog his tennis ball. 'If all else fails, I'll get her liquored up before we come here and she'll think he's the best dog since Rin Tin Tin.'

'Aye, just make sure that's all she sees if you get her pished and bring her here.'

'Deary me, Bob. Such a glass-half-empty outlook on life.'

Just then, the lounge door opened and Detective Superintendent Kara Page poked her head in. 'Is your son always a heavy sleeper?'

'I don't think so. But he was out on the lash...I

mean, he was having a sociable drink with a friend of his last night.'

'I'll go and give him a knock,' Bob said, and he left the room and clumped upstairs. He returned a few minutes later. 'No joy. I'll go and get the spare key, just in case he's injured or something.'

'He's not answering his phone either,' Kara said.

'He should get a dog like me. Less trouble and they don't keep you out all night.'

'Dogs don't buy a round, though, do they?' Kara said.

'Or get a spider out of the bath. In case you were wondering if you should get a dog when you move into your new place.'

'I think I can manage to deal with a spider,' she replied. 'It's men who get on my wick.'

Max dropped the ball and looked at Ed expectantly. Ed picked it up and put it in his pocket. He was starting to have doubts about bringing his new floozy home in case Max got on *her* wick. On a romantic level of between one and ten, a face being washed by a dog's slobbery tongue after he'd licked his balls was minus twenty. Probably be best if they went back to her hotel then.

'Got them,' Bob said, coming back with the spare keys, and the three of them went up the stairs. Max followed behind, alternating between looking at the stairs and looking for his tennis ball, and then darted past and reached the landing before Ed. He sat down, looking at Ed.

'Now you sit. I'm sure somewhere down the line one of your relatives was a chocolate lab.' Ed tossed the ball for Max.

'I hope he isn't in there with Chaz having an early-morning sesh,' Bob said.

'Drinking at this hour?' Kara said.

'No, I meant –'

'She knows what you mean, Bob,' Ed said.

'Oh aye, right.'

Kara grinned at the ex-detective's discomfort.

Bob fumbled with the key for a moment, then knocked again. 'Sean? You in there?' *Answer, ya bastard.*

He turned the key in the lock and opened the door. 'Fire!' he shouted, before seeing the bed hadn't been slept in.

Another door opened along the hallway. 'Is there a fire?' Natalie Hogan said, coming out of her room while pulling on a robe.

'No, no, it's alright,' Bob said, coming out of Bracken's room again.

Another guest opened the door further along. An old man who was visiting Edinburgh for a few days with his wife. 'Hurry up, Dorothy! The place is well alight!'

'No, it's fine,' Bob said. 'No fire.'

Alec adjusted his hearing aid and let out a shriek. 'Fire, Dorothy! We're going to die!'

Bob stepped closer and waved his hands in front of the panicking old man. Max started barking. 'Alec, it's a false alarm. There's no fire.'

Alec stopped in his tracks as his wife appeared at the door trying unsuccessfully to get her false teeth in.

'Why have you got the fire dog then?' Alec said, pointing to the big dog, who was lying down on his front, chewing on his tennis ball.

'Fire dog?' Bob said. 'What the bloody hell's a fire dog when he's at home?'

'Alec, I need to pee,' Dorothy said round the false teeth.

'I think I already have,' Alec replied, looking down at the front of his pyjama bottoms to confirm that his trip to the bathroom was now unwarranted. 'No, wait, I haven't, but now I'm touching cloth. And you,' he said to Bob, 'you should be farking ashamed.'

'Alec! What have I told you about swearing?' Dorothy said, her tongue so sharp she could have cut the Christmas turkey with it.

'*Farking* isn't swearing.'

'We all know what you meant,' Dorothy said through a mouthful of plastic.

'Sorry, folks,' Bob said, but two bedroom doors closed on his apology.

'Bloody fire,' Kara said. 'Don't go shouting that at the pictures next time you're there.'

'I was trying to wake his nibs up. Waste of time because his bed hasn't been slept in.'

Kara looked at Ed. 'You said your son was out with a friend last night? Do you think he got caught up in an all-nighter?'

That'd better be all the wee bastard was doing. 'I'm not sure, Kara, love. Maybe things got out of hand. Maybe he's in the Royal Infirmary.' *He will be by the time I'm finished with him.*

'If he's not answering his phone, how will we get in touch with him?' Kara asked.

'I might have his friend's phone number some-where,' Ed said, not elaborating on how he would have the contact details. He took Max and went up the back stairs to his own room at the top of the house.

FIVE

Bracken woke up to the sound of somebody moving about in his room. He tried to straighten his legs out but couldn't. Surely Chaz hadn't stayed over last night? He couldn't remember even asking her to come over after he got home.

The curtains were holding back a damp morning, but Bracken couldn't see it yet. His eyes were sticky and thick and he blinked a few times, trying to get some moisture going in them. Bastard things weren't cooperating. The light got brighter the more he opened his eyes, but he couldn't focus on anything. Wasn't that the start of cataracts? Christ, he would lose his job if he couldn't see.

Blinking so fast he could have been using Morse code, he tried sitting up to rub them, but his head shouted at him: *Whoa there. And just what the hell do you think you're doing?* Pain shot him in the head, just behind the eyes. He laid his head back down on the pillow. Why couldn't he stretch his legs out? He never tucked his sheets in, even in winter, so he would be able to stretch and kick them off if he got too hot.

'Morning, sleepyhead,' a voice said from somewhere. Christ, he'd died and now his mother was talking to him.

Exaggerated eye movements cleared his vision enough to see the Angel of Mercy standing above him, upside down. She was smiling, so maybe his death had been silent and swift. Not exactly pain free, what with his head being the way it was.

Angel walked round, holding something in her hand.

'Coffee and a couple of painkillers,' Catherine said, putting the mug on the coffee table next to him.

Then it all came back to him. A few tinnies in Catherine's flat, followed by some Glayva chasers. Then just the Glayva, on the rocks, followed by some Baileys Irish Cream when he'd arsed the Glayva.

'What time is it?' he asked her, finally managing to sit up without feeling like his head was about to fall off.

'Just gone eight thirty.'

'What? Oh God, why didn't you wake me?'

'Because you sleep like the dead when you're blootered. I know from experience.'

He was wearing his t-shirt from the night before –
just that and his underpants, he noticed as the blanket
fell off. He grabbed it and pulled it over his lower half.

'Take your painkillers and have your coffee. Then
you can have a shower. There's a change of clothing on
my bed. Clean shirt and underwear. Fresh t-shirt.'

'How...?'

'I told you the last time you crashed on my couch
that I'd get a change of clothes for you. One casual, one
for work. There's a choice of ties.'

'Just as well I wasn't relying on using some of
Leon's clothes.'

'Despite your ramblings last night, he isn't a
midget, circus variety or otherwise. Yes, he's only five-
six, and yes, it would have been funny to watch you
climb into his trousers, but he doesn't keep any clothes
here.'

Bracken swallowed the painkillers. God, the coffee
was good. He felt the hot liquid wash down his gullet.
Catherine always could make a good coffee. The one
first thing in the morning was always the best.

'How come you don't look "neither up nor down"?'
he asked her, seeing she was already dressed for work
in her business suit.

'The Grand Old Duke of York reminded me I was
working today, so I quit early. It slowly dwindled to a
party of one. Never trust a stranger with your heart.'

Bracken looked puzzled.

'Kim Wilde. You said you liked her voice and played that track about five times. I think there was some subliminal message there about Leon and me. You know, like when you play an album backwards and some creepy voice tells you to go fuck yourself.'

'I like Kim's voice. "Never Trust a Stranger" is my favourite track of hers.'

'Again, subliminal message. About Leon's impending marriage proposal.'

Bracken didn't want to get into a fight, so he just drank more of his coffee. 'Where does he live?' he asked his ex.

'Across the road, round the corner there. Sandport.' She told him the number.

'You ever go there?'

'No. He's always here. Which suits me. I'm already home, so I don't have to walk home in the rain.'

Catherine's phone rang and she left the living room to answer it. 'Hello, Dad,' he heard her say.

He knew Catherine's father was dead, so unless she was talking to him through a medium or her phone had some magical powers, he knew who was on the other end and why.

Catherine came back into the room. 'It's for you.' She held out her phone.

'Take a message. Please. I don't want to hear the old sod lecturing me.'

She put the phone back to her ear. Listened to the other end. 'He says he can hear you,' she said to Bracken.

'Tell him I'm glad he doesn't need to get his hearing checked.'

'Do you want me to just put him on speakerphone?'

'Tell him I'll call him later.'

'He'll call you later, Dad. I have to run. I'm working this morning...Okay, I will. Bye...Love you too.'

Catherine had her *you owe me* grin on. 'He says it's not him you have to worry about. Kara's on the warpath too.'

He stood up, letting the blanket fall down.

'God, all we need is for Leon to walk in right now,' Catherine said. 'Go shower.'

He walked through to the bathroom. 'Toothbrush?'

'On the sink. I bought a new one and kept it in my drawer.'

'I owe you one, Cath.'

'I know you do,' she said.

'Did Sarah leave for uni already?'

'She stayed overnight with a friend. She'll be back tonight.'

'Tell her I said hi.'

'I'm going, Sean. You still got your emergency key to lock my door?'

'I have.'

'See you later.'

She let herself out, and Bracken showered and dressed. When he was done, he stood looking out of Catherine's living room window. He wondered if Leon was down there, looking back. It wasn't something he was going to worry about.

He switched his phone back on and there was a text from Kara Page with an address south of Edinburgh.

Be there! Soon, Sean. I mean it.

He dialled a number. 'Jimmy?' DI Jimmy Sullivan.

'Yes, boss?'

'I'm a bit under the weather, son. Could you come and pick me up?'

'No problem. Where?'

He thought on his feet for a moment. 'There's a wee café at the Shore. Near Sandport Place. I'll be there.'

'I'll be as quick as I can. Better I use the blues. We got a shout.'

'Whatever it takes.'

He hung up, and for the first time in a while, he felt happy.

SIX

'What's Gaelic for shitehole again?' Stewie Anderson said as he stumbled on the overgrown driveway, nearly falling. 'Sake.'

Stella Mason laughed. 'Do that again, but wait until I get my phone out. I can shove it up on YouTube.'

'And I can shove it up your arse.'

'Why are you in such a shitty mood today?'

Stewie held his hands out as if he was trying to catch the rain. 'If I close my eyes, I can almost feel like I'm in the Bahamas.'

'I think you need a wee break or something, Stewie.'

'Why couldn't it have rained last night? Those wee bastards were lighting squibs and firing them into our stair. The dug nearly shat himself. I'd put a rocket up their fucking arse, so I would. Bloody useless clowns in the Parliament allowing kids to play with explosives, I ask you.' He turned to look at her. 'This is just breeding domestic terrorists; you mark my words.'

'Maybe you should try and get out a bit more, Stewie. Get a girlfriend.'

'The last thing I want in my life right now is another woman.'

They stopped and looked at the decrepit house, the paint peeling off in patches on the outside walls like it had some sort of disease.

'Why would anybody want to buy this craphole?' Stewie wondered again. He'd wondered it the first time they'd come here to check it out, he'd wondered it when they'd got in Stella's car today, and he'd wondered it when they'd turned onto the dirt road to drive up here. He was more than giving a broken record a run for its money.

'The couple come from London. The money they'll spend on this place is probably a drop in the ocean to them.'

Stewie and Stella were property managers for a new property show called *Diamond in the Rough*, hosted by Desmond Rough. Or as Stewie called him, *that obnoxious wank*.

'This is just taking the piss out of the viewers. They have to sit through all that drivel while the new owners *ooh* and *aah* over the properties before picking one. Only the viewer doesn't know this is the one they've already picked.'

'It's going to be a good show, Stewie. It keeps us in a job. At least while they film the first series.'

'Aye, but it's all the mince we have to go through. Don't drive too close to the house, so the driveway looks undisturbed. Don't take a piss anywhere on the property.' He turned to Stella. 'Talking of disturbed, that ponce Desmond better start showing respect to the crew. After five episodes, you'd think he would know he's a baw hair away from getting decked. I heard Tony, one of the cameramen, say he was going to, and I quote, "knock that fairy bastard on his arse".'

'Desmond's just under pressure. Working with people who aren't actors, people who've never been in front of a camera before except to take a picture of themselves naked to send in a message.'

Stewie actually smiled at that. 'I remember back in the day, you had to use a Polaroid instant camera to take a photo of your dick to send to somebody.'

'I don't remember that because I never had one of those cameras. That's disgusting.'

'I never had one either. I just read about it somewhere.' He hurriedly turned away from her and stood looking at the dilapidated house. 'Shithole,' he said again, walking forward.

'You did remember the key?' Stella asked him.

'Duh. Yes, Miss Mason. You think I'm a right spaz at times.'

'It wouldn't be the first time you've forgotten a key, twat.'

Stewie looked at the hills in the distance, shrouded in clouds now. The rain was a fine drizzle, the kind that made you think it wasn't much but then gave you a good belting, soaking you through to your underpants. You had to get out of it before you got drenched. That was the excuse he'd used the last time he had his trousers round his knees while having a pish down a close off Edinburgh's High Street.

Just sheltering from the rain, Officer.

Wi' yer fuckin' knob oot?

The police officer had hardly given him time to pull his trousers back up before he'd started chasing him, much less buckle his belt. He'd still managed to outrun the fat bastard.

This time, the clothing they were wearing was meant to protect them from the elements.

They turned when they heard a shout from behind them.

'Oh, I say! Mr Stewie, wait up.'

'Aw, here's that fucking toff,' Stewie said as the Land Rover pulled up.

Bernie Appleton had been born into the big-silverspoon machine and pooped out of Eton years later, with a polished accent and an attitude to match. According to his own flatulence-enhanced stories. Stewie wasn't so much a cad and bounder, but more like a ruffian footman who shouldn't forget his place in life.

Appleton was the production company's rep, and he enjoyed letting everybody know it. He was a small man but made up for it with a big voice.

Then the passenger door opened.

'Oh, Christ, he's with Sir Ponce-a-Lot,' Stewie said, screwing his face up when he saw Desmond Rough himself.

'Nothing like a good old bracing walk in the Scottish hills, is there?' Appleton said.

'I could think of better places to be right now than having the Scottish weather pish down on me,' Stewie answered.

'I passed a homeless man on Princes Street the other day. There but for the grace of God go you and I, Stewie. This job pays the bills, I'm sure.' Appleton was breathing hard now, the walk from the driveway further down akin to climbing Mount Everest for a fat bastard like him.

'You should have asked him if he wanted to come on board,' Stewie said.

Appleton tutted and walked past him. 'Come on,

Stella, let's see what this place has in store for us.'

Stella looked over her shoulder and grinned as Stewie stuck two fingers up behind Appleton's back.

'Wait up!' Rough shouted.

Stewie made a face like a dog smelling its own vomit. 'If he wasn't such a lassie about getting his shoes dirty, he would be up here by now. Look at him, scared he'll break a fucking fingernail.'

They approached the door, and Desmond was trying to keep his breathing even but failing miserably.

'God, these hills would cripple a goat.' Despite being from Edinburgh originally, Rough spoke with a southern accent, like he had gone to school in England.

'Coming through. VIP on the scene. Hangers-on, beware,' Stewie said, shoving past them.

'Deary me, you are in a strop today, aren't you?' Appleton said.

'Aw, fuck off,' Stewie said.

'I beg your pardon?'

'Some fucknut's broken the door. Look, the lock's gone tits-up.' Stewie knew bad language got under Appleton's skin and did his best to rile the older man at every opportunity.

'I hope it's not some of those foreign buggers who come here and think it's okay to break out the spray paint,' Appleton said.

Stewie turned to look at him. 'Foreign buggers?'

'You know what I mean. Those bloody gypsies. Steal your eyesight if it wasn't nailed down.'

Rough nodded in agreement.

Pair of bastards, thought Stewie. This was why Stewie's job wasn't in any peril from Appleton: homophobic, xenophobic and quite a few other –phobics thrown in for good measure.

Stewie nudged the door with his boot and could almost feel Appleton's stinky breath on his neck.

'Ease up there, Bernie. You're almost up my arse.' An observation *and* a slur on his character all in one go. He was sure Stella would be proud of him. If she was even paying attention. She wasn't drunk and she wasn't high, something she would rectify later on in the day.

Suddenly, Stewie turned round to look at Rough. 'Listen, if there are some gyppo bastards in there, I need to know you're with me if push comes to shove.' Meaning: *If I fucking shove you towards some raging fuck with bad teeth who's swinging an axe, you're going to get in about him. While me and Stella make our escape.*

'Of course I've got your back,' Appleton said in a way that was most unconvincing. 'I mean, I'll call the police for a start, don't you worry about that. Bloody breaking and entering. This is not some backward EU country, let me tell you.'

All Appleton needed now was some racist comments and he'd be playing with a full deck.

'Don't worry, I'll take one for the team,' Rough said.

'I bet you would,' Stewie said in a low voice.

'What?'

'Nothing.' Stewie looked to see if Appleton had heard, but if he had, he gave no indication. 'Right then. Stella, watch our backs. Me and Robert the Bruce are going in.'

Stewie sidestepped, reached behind Appleton and shoved him from the hallway into the living room.

The older man screamed and Stewie burst out laughing. 'There's fuck all in here to steal. Why would some gypsy come in here?' he shouted.

But Appleton wouldn't stop screaming.

'Jesus, Bernie, I'm only having a laugh,' Stewie said, stepping into the room, Rough right behind him.

Then he saw what Appleton was screaming at.

And it wasn't a gypsy.

SEVEN

To give DI Jimmy Sullivan his due, he hadn't asked why Bracken was being picked up at the Shore. Bracken knew the younger man was dying to ask him, but he was making small talk at the moment.

'So, the wife wants to go away at Christmas, maybe Tenerife, somewhere warm like that. I said to her, what about our parents, they wouldn't see the kids? So she said, they can see them before we go. Right bloody palaver, so it is.'

Bracken's head was still on the final approach. He knew it would make it to see the arse end of the morning, but right now it was still up in the air. He was sitting in the passenger seat with his eyes closed tackling a conundrum: would he shoot a man who was pointing a rifle at Sullivan right now, or would Bracken shoot Sullivan first? Anything to make him stop fucking talking.

'You're not sleeping, I can tell,' Sullivan said.

'I never said I was. I'm just resting my eyes until we get there. Waiting for the flight attendant to come round and serve breakfast. What time did the captain say we'll be landing?'

'It's not my fault the traffic's heavy this morning.'

'Stick the blues back on. All the coffee I've had this morning, I may or may not be about to take a piss at the next traffic light. And that wouldn't look too good on my annual review.'

'Why didn't you say so?' Sullivan said.

'I didn't think I had to, Jimmy, considering you came hooring down from Great Junction Street like you're on fucking glue. One American tourist in the café thought we were filming an episode of *Get Back, Ya Bastard*.'

'Never heard of that show. I don't watch crime shows, since we get enough of it in real life.'

'It's a kids' show.'

The siren jolted Bracken for a moment and the car turned suddenly to the right. Bracken banged his head off the passenger window.

'Fuck's sake,' he said, hoping the dunt wasn't going to make his headache worse. He didn't know where they were and didn't want to open his eyes to find out.

The rain had stopped and another one of Edinburgh's 'four seasons in one day' had stepped up. The sun was out now, trying its best to blind him. His request to borrow sunglasses from Sullivan had been met with scorn and the question, 'Sunglasses in November?'

'Just wait till it's bouncing off the wet road and blinding you, sarky bastard,' Bracken had said.

The heat in the car had gripped him from the word go, and now he felt himself succumbing to it. The siren was hardly a lullaby, but the wailing was actually sending him off.

He didn't know how long he had been asleep, but when he woke up there were no buildings around, just a wooden-fenced pen holding cars instead of sheep. A stone tower rose into the air in the distance.

'Where are we?' he asked.

'Outside Penicuik. Heading to Silverburn, remember?'

'No need to get uppity, Inspector.'

'Not getting uppity, sir. Just pointing out a fact.'

'I'm not quite there yet this morning.'

'I've always thought you're not all there.'

'Cheeky bastard. That's not what I said.'

He yawned and closed his eyes to rest them for a moment. When they'd had a suitable amount of R and R, he opened them again and noticed the siren was off now. When it had been switched off, he couldn't say.

'The rest of the team there?'

'Already in situ.'

Bracken had noticed Sullivan using big words and Latin phrases recently, like he had discovered some secret code. All it did was make him look like a swot, and Bracken didn't like it.

'Is that a yes?'

Sullivan took his eyes off the road for a second, a frown creasing his face.

'Yes, I do know what it means. Do you think they hand out promotions to gullible twats who don't know how to spell their name without looking it up in a telephone directory?'

'I wasn't suggesting anything.'

'What's Latin for *keep your fucking eyes on the road*?'

'*Oculos...via...*something. I don't know what *fuck* is in Latin.'

'It was rhetorical, Jimmy. *Maximus anus.*'

'I'm not even sure that's Latin. I think you're just taking the piss out of me now.'

'What gave it away?'

They were heading to Silverburn, a dot on the map on the A702, Edinburgh to West Linton. They crossed over the main road and went up a narrow country road,

then turned right through a wooden gate and drove up
a rough track where there was a slew of police vehicles
and an ambulance.

Sullivan stopped the car and they got out into the
cold air. The sun was gone and the drizzle had started
again.

'Chaz is here,' Sullivan said.

Bracken was silent for a moment before looking at
Sullivan. 'I'm not asking you to lie –'

'About me picking you up near your ex-wife's
house?'

'Why don't you shout it a bit louder? There's a
shepherd over the side of that mountain didn't quite
catch it.' Bracken tutted and shook his head as they
walked toward the house. 'I'm not asking you to lie, just
not to volunteer any information. It's a complicated
story as to why I was there. And it wasn't anything
mucky, so get your head out of the gutter.'

'I never said a word.' They carried on past a Range
Rover and a small foreign hatchback that was on its
way to the scrapyard.

'What do you think of Chaz staying at the
mortuary instead of moving to the Sick Kids'?' Sullivan
asked.

'After the shenanigans that went on at the mortuary, they're lucky to have her. And now there's always
two on call at night. I think she's happier than she

would be working in a lab in a hospital. And they gave her a pay increase, so now she's on more than she would have been getting if she'd left.'

'How's the house-hunting going?'

Bracken had told the DI that once again somebody had stepped in and offered more money on the flat he was after.

'I need to offer more money, I think. The house prices in Edinburgh are ridiculous.'

'Still not taking Chaz up on her offer to move into her place?'

'It's a sticky wicket, Jimmy. I move in, then I'm no longer king of my own castle. The queen will rule the kingdom and I won't have a say. Does that make sense?'

Sullivan laughed. 'Perfectly. I moved in with a woman before I met the wife. She'd bought the place. Her fiancé had cheated on her and she'd kicked him out because the flat was hers. I moved in and it was like moving into a lair. I couldn't do anything I wanted. Couldn't put my feet up on the coffee table. She booted me out shortly after that.'

'That's fucking manky anyway. What if you stood in dog shite then put your feet on the table where you put your coffee mug? I'd have booted you out for that, no problem.'

'Besides that, I couldn't lie in on a day off. If she was up, I had to be up. I couldn't go to the pub with my mates. She wanted me all to herself. It was such a relief when she told me to pack my bags.'

'Where'd you go?' Bracken asked as they got closer to the house.

'My ma's house of course. Iron my own shirt? That was another bloody thing.'

'And now we get down to the nitty-gritty. Jimmy Sullivan didn't want to iron his own shirts. That's being a sexist bastard, if you don't mind me saying.'

'I do mind actually. It wasn't being sexist. I used to pay my ma to do my laundry and iron my shirts.' Sullivan looked at Bracken. 'Who does yours?'

'Never mind who does my shirts. It's not Chaz. Let's leave it at that.'

'Mary then.'

'I pay Mary to do my laundry, if you must know.'

Sullivan grinned. 'I knew it.'

DS Izzie Khan was standing off to one side, next to DS Tam Gale. They were talking with three other people. Izzie made the introductions as Bracken approached.

'Sir, this is Desmond Rough, the show's presenter. Stella Mason and Stewie Anderson, property consultants.'

'Surely I don't need an introduction?' Rough said, making a face.

'Who found the body?' Bracken asked, dispensing with any niceties.

'I did,' Rough said. 'Well, Bernie was first in, but I was right behind.' Bracken noticed the little man was the only one wearing a suit, albeit under a Barbour waxed jacket.

'Tell me what happened,' Bracken said, taking the man aside with Sullivan.

'I nearly had to take a piss in my boxers,' Rough said. 'We went into the house, just to have a look around, as we're about to start filming here, and that woman was in the chair.'

'The three of you went in at the same time?'

'There were four of us. My colleague Bernie Appleton was here as well. He was taken to the Royal in shock. But yes, me in the lead, and that...fucking *thing* was sitting staring at me. Through the plastic bag. Then we all booted it out of there and I called the police.'

'When was the last time you were here?'

'This is my first time. I've never set eyes on this place except in photos.'

'And Appleton's job is?' Bracken asked.

'He oversees the properties for the production company.'

'And those two?' Bracken nodded towards the younger man and woman.

'They're hired as property managers for the show. They make sure there are no hurdles by the time we're ready to start filming.'

'What's the show?' Sullivan asked.

'*Diamond in the Rough.* With me, Desmond Rough. You heard of me?'

'No,' Bracken said.

'I have,' Sullivan said. 'My wife watches that show. Is this what this is?'

'I just said so, didn't I?' Rough said.

'Run me through what happens on the show,' Bracken said as Sullivan turned away, barely containing the word 'wanker'.

Rough dug his hands further into the pockets of his Barbour. 'We follow a couple as they look at old properties that are dying on their feet. Abandoned but with potential. They look at three and pick one, then we follow them as they bring the property back to life. But what the audience doesn't know is, they've already picked out a property with our help. The other two properties are just smoke and mirrors. This is the house that they chose.'

'How long ago did they buy it?'

'The contract was signed a month ago. Filming is due to begin next week. This was the final look-over before the production crew start to bring their gear up.'

'How many people knew about this being the property?'

'Only the main production staff. Management. Those two.' Rough nodded in the direction of the two young people. 'If I was you, I would start with the man. Stewie Anderson. Right lowlife.'

'Did you recognise the woman in the chair?' Bracken asked.

'She had a bag over her head. I don't know about you, Chief Inspector, but I don't go with women who need to have a bag put over their head before we get down to business. I mean, some of them have come close, but a few drinks sorted that.'

'Do you know the victim?' Bracken asked.

'Again, bag over the head. She could be *your* wife for all I know.'

Bracken clenched his jaw for a second. Better than breaking this toffee-nosed bastard's.

'We'll need you to go to the station to make a formal statement. We might want to ask you some more questions, but you can leave your details with one of my other officers.' So *we can run you through our system to see if you're some kind of sick fuck.*

Bracken walked over to the house and let on to Tam Gale, who was talking to the young man. A voice was being raised. It was the man shouting, not Gale.

Tam Gale was an older detective who had risen to the rank of sergeant by sheer luck.

'Jimmy, go and see what's going on there while I go into the house,' Bracken said.

'Sure, boss.'

Sullivan walked away while Bracken entered the house. *Diamond in the Rough* wasn't quite cutting it. *Shitehole in the Wild* was more like it. Forensics had put in arc lights, making the scene look like something from a horror movie.

'Scene one, we have Sherlock entering stage left,' Chaz Cullen said. 'And...action!'

'You're hilarious,' he said.

Chaz stood grinning at him. 'Hey, if I'd gone to work in the lab, there would be no hilarity at work, would there?' she said.

'I suppose not. Life would indeed be boring.'

'We're lucky you stayed,' Jim Brown said. He was a younger bloke who was relatively new to the mortuary team.

'I know,' Chaz replied, grinning.

'Calm down there, or else you won't be able to get your head out of the tent.' Brown chuckled.

Dr Pamela Green was examining the woman sitting in the chair and Bracken could see right away that the victim's legs were badly burned. The room was empty, with no signs of there having been any furniture in here for a long time. It smelled stale and some of the wallpaper was peeling off. Whatever had once been a carpet had given up the ghost and died a peaceful death a long time ago.

'Hi, Sean. Is this young woman bothering you?' Pamela asked.

'Not any more than usual.'

'Oh, I see how it's going,' Chaz said. 'My boyfriend avoided my calls last night, and today he's taking the side of the good doctor. Interesting.'

He didn't answer and avoided eye contact. 'What's the story so far, Pam?'

'I cut the bag off her head. It was clear, and taped round her neck.'

'What about the legs?'

Pam turned to face him and straightened her back, making a face. 'Not getting any younger for this stuff.' She stretched her back again. 'This poor woman's legs were set on fire. They used an accelerant. Obviously. To have burn marks like this.'

'Could that have been the cause of death? Like, she died from being in so much pain?'

'Could be. I've seen people die from shock. However, I can't determine that until I get her on the table. The bag might be the cause.'

Bracken looked past the pathologist and saw the

victim's arms were still on the arms of the metal chair, held in place by cable ties.

'She wasn't killed here,' he said matter-of-factly.

'You're right,' Pam answered.

'No detritus under the chair from having her legs burned,' he said, looking at the discoloured face.

'The cable ties are there to hold her in place. He wanted her sitting upright, facing the door, when somebody came in.'

'Any ID on her?' Bracken asked.

'No, nothing,' Chaz answered. 'Her prints look pretty intact, so we can have them in the system by the end of the morning. That'll give your bloodshot eyes time to focus,' she said, grinning.

'Remind me to wear sunglasses in future,' he answered. 'Any idea of TOD?'

'I'm guessing three to four days.'

'Thanks, Pam.' He turned round and made for the door.

He got out into the cold air; the drizzle was taking a tea break, it seemed. Chaz came right out behind him.

'Did I do something to annoy you?' she asked him.

'What? Oh no, of course not,' he said, half-facing her.

Her paper suit rustled as she stepped round in front of him.

'Why didn't you text me last night? You usually do.

When you didn't, I sent you one, but there was no reply.'

'Oh, it was nothing. I had a drink with an old friend and things got out of hand. Well, not out of hand in the debauchery kind of way, but I had too much to drink.'

'I thought that's what it would be. I almost called Ed.'

A scene flashed through Bracken's head just then: Ed answering the phone and telling Chaz that his son was out gallivanting with his ex-wife.

He didn't reply.

'As long as we're still good,' she said.

'Of course we are. Things will be different when I get my own place.'

'Maybe come round for a bite to eat tonight? Watch a film or something?'

'I'd like that.' He smiled at her.

'See you later, Alligator.'

He walked away, wondering if she was expecting an *In a while, Crocodile,* but he would have felt like a real twat saying that while there were other people milling about.

'Their story is pretty much the same as the older bloke's,' Sullivan said, walking up to Bracken. 'They were here checking on the property and they found the dead girl inside, sitting on that chair.'

'Get them to come into the station and make a statement. Run them all through the system. I want to know if any of them have any priors.'

'Will do.'

Bracken turned back to look at the house, but there was no sign of Chaz.

Had she seen through his lie? Was it really a lie? No, it hadn't been a lie. He just hadn't elaborated, that was all.

Yeah, keep telling yourself that, Bracken.

EIGHT

Bracken's mouth felt like he'd been licking a kitchen floor. He was sitting across from Kara Page at her desk and he could feel himself dozing off, the heat was up so high.

'You look like shite, Sean.'

'Shite Sean. That sounds like my superhero name.' There was a little plastic cup of water sitting in front of him on her desk. It was doing nothing to quench his thirst. The alcohol was conspiring to rob his body of whatever water was floating around inside.

'How was your night out with your friend?' she said. She was sitting back in her chair, her fingers clasped in front of her.

'I was helping somebody with a problem. The drinking got out of hand. I've not been driving, though, if that's what you're worried about.'

'I'm not. You're probably a better driver pished than Jimmy Sullivan is sober. I was just worried that something was wrong when you weren't down for breakfast this morning.'

Bracken was quiet for a moment. Kara had become a friend since she had moved into the guest house, but no boundaries had ever been crossed, either professionally or privately.

'I'm a big boy, ma'am.'

'I know you are, but the good folks at the Glenlivet guest house were all rooting for you to be on this side of the Accident and Emergency department. Especially your dad.'

'Oh, God. The old man wasn't nipping your head about me, was he?'

'Not at all. He was doing some dog training this morning.'

'Oh, yes. He did mention he has a date with a hot female and he wants to show off his obedient canine.'

'He wasn't having much luck.'

'I bet. He spoils that dog. He should have just told her he was rich. That's what I would have done.'

'And when he takes her back to the guest house for afternoon tea?' Kara said.

Bracken let that little nugget sit for a second. 'He wouldn't take her back there.'

'He's planning on doing just that. They're going

out on a date and he's taking her back to the guest house.'

'At least we know he's going to behave himself.'

'Now we've established that you would lie to a woman, I think Ed has the better morals between the two of you.'

'That's just an impression he likes to give.'

Kara sat up. 'But anyway, bring me up to speed on this murder we have on our hands.'

Bracken sipped the water before putting the cup down on the desk. 'The house has just been bought by a couple moving up from London, Mr and Mrs Cliff Robertson.'

'The ones who are taking part in this show. What's it called again?'

'Diamond in the Rough.'

'God, yes, with the blow-hard Desmond Rough,' Kara said. 'Not one of my favourite TV hosts.'

'Overpaid ponce. According to one of the witnesses, Stewie Anderson. I heard him talking to Tam Gale as they were going to an interview room for Anderson to give his statement.'

'Has he been interviewed yet?' Kara asked. 'Rough, I mean.'

'At the crime scene. The other one who was there, Bernie Appleton, was taken to the Royal in shock. I'll send Tam Gale and young Lennox Docherty to interview him, but I'm not sure how much use he'll be. It's not going to slow down production, apparently.'

'Christ, don't tell me they're still going ahead with the show, Sean?'

'Rough is adamant. A few people have sunk a lot of money into this series and they'll only see a return on their investment if the show goes ahead. But not until we clear it as a crime scene.'

'And it won't do ratings any harm if the viewers know that's where the body of a young woman was found.'

'Rough did seem a bit pleased with that prospect.'

'When you get a firmer time of death, make sure your team checks out the alibis.'

'Will do.'

'Have the backgrounds been started on those who found the body yet?' she asked.

'Yes. Nothing's showing up. We'll dig deeper.'

'How long has the house been empty?' Kara asked.

'Five years. The bones of the building are good, but the idea of the show is to get an old dump and turn it into a palace.'

'Who was the last owner?'

'An old couple. The wife died first, then when the old man went, the family held on to it.'

'And they let it fall into disrepair?'

'They wanted to sell it, but they couldn't trace one

of the siblings. The guy was off backpacking around the world. It sat empty for years, and it's suspected that people gained entry into it and sheltered there, although you would think it was halfway up Ben Nevis. Windows were left open and the rot started. I was told that the sibling was eventually contacted and the family put the house up for sale around eight months ago. It didn't sell and it was eventually spotted by the production company, who had the owners in a contract by then, and it was bought and was to be featured on the show.'

Kara nodded. 'What about the prints from the victim?'

'She's not in the system.'

'She wasn't burnt up at that house but somewhere else. Then transported there. I don't think he came upon that house by chance. I mean, he was driving about with a corpse in his vehicle, then he took her in there to stage the scene for when she would be found. It could be either somebody who knew that house had been for sale or somebody connected to the production company.'

'That's what we're thinking. The house is too isolated to be picked at random.'

'Okay, Sean. Keep me in the loop.'

'Will do, ma'am.' Bracken stood up and picked up the cup of water.

'Oh, and one more thing, Sean.'

'Yes?'

'If you're playing with fire, please make sure that Chaz doesn't get burned.'

'I'm not playing with fire.' *Skating on thin ice, but there's no fire involved.*

'Good.'

He left the office and went back to the incident room.

'I'm thinking we might have to bring the press in on this,' Jimmy Sullivan said. 'They already have wind that something is up. It won't be long before they start crawling all over it. We could have a digital image made up of the victim and give it to them. Maybe somebody could identify her.'

'Claire Thompson,' Izzie Khan said, turning from her computer.

Bracken and the others looked at her.

'Been missing since last Wednesday. She comes from Fife.'

NINE

Driving back over to the Kingdom of Fife always felt like going home for Bracken. He'd enjoyed living here for six years. There had seemed less hassle here than in Edinburgh. And his dad had lived in a mobile home up from Hillend, and he had popped over for a beer now and again.

Now he was heading back to Glenrothes to see his former DI, Cameron Robb. The clouds had moved along, obviously bored now of pishing down on people. But they'd be back with a vengeance. Normally, Bracken would have taken a drive through the little fishing villages up the coast, but today was all business, so he booted it up the A92 to Glenrothes and the police HQ for Fife.

He pulled up in front of the modern brown-stone

building in Detroit Road, parking the car at the front door.

Inside, he saw a few familiar faces, one of them his old boss, DSup Benny Gladstone.

'Well, well, the fucking bad penny and all that,' Gladstone said as Bracken was ushered through the back.

'You knew I wouldn't be able to stay away,' Bracken said, smiling and shaking the man's proffered hand.

'Time for a tea?' the older detective said.

'When have you ever known me to refuse such hospitality, sir?'

'Never. Mind you, I've had to cut back on the doughnuts. As you can see.' Gladstone patted his gut. 'I've lost twenty-three grams. But I'm sticking to it. The doc said I was on my way to having a blocked carotid. Like my old man. His was blocked ninety per cent when he dropped down of a stroke. Poor old sod. He liked his dairy cream cakes, but what the hell? He was eighty years old. Why would he want to take care of himself?'

Bracken couldn't fault that logic, except Gladstone was in his mid-fifties.

They walked along the corridor to Gladstone's office.

'You get to a certain age, you have to think: I've had a good life, let's get wired into the cakes,' Bracken said.

'Exactly. He died a happy man. I mean, his dream was to die on top of a prossie, but we can't have everything we want in life. Am I right?'

'Spot on, sir.'

Gladstone hesitated. 'You know what, let's go to the canteen. I have a wee kettle, but I'm a selfish bastard when it comes to dishing out my teabags.'

They started walking again.

'You don't have one of those fancy coffee machines?' Bracken asked.

'Whit? One of those over-priced recycled Heinz Beans cans? No, thank you. I wouldn't want one of those. Give me a good old kettle any day of the week. Preferably like the one my granny used to have. Whistle its baws off, it would, sitting on her cooker.'

'I remember those. My granny had one too.'

'Aye, she went a bit doolally in the end. She put a piece of cheese-on-toast on the grill and sat down to watch some shite on the TV and forgot it was on. Set the bloody cooker on fire. Luckily, a neighbour saw the smoke coming out of her house, but by then it was too late. The bloody place was well up. The neighbour got her out just in time.'

'Thank God the neighbour was there, sir.'

'Aye. She lived another four years after that.'

Gladstone went into the canteen and Bracken

followed, noticing a few of the uniforms sitting at tables. A couple smiled and let on to him.

'I'll get the teas,' Bracken said, putting his hand in his pocket.

'Wow, look at you, Big Spender.'

'I have to splash out now and again, sir.'

'Aye, you can't take it with you, son.'

They sat down with their teas.

'Christ, listen to me today, all doom and gloom. This job is getting to me, Sean. Retirement is calling. This job gets on my tits at times. Talking of which...'

DI Cameron Robb had walked into the canteen. Bracken was genuinely pleased to see the younger man.

'Refill, sir?' Robb asked.

'We've just sat down, son' Gladstone said. 'Grab yourself one and join us. See if there's any doughnuts.'

'You just said you were giving them up,' Bracken said.

'Cutting down on them, I believe I said. There's a difference.'

Robb got his tea and sat down at the table. 'No doughnuts.'

'You didn't try very hard, eh? There's a Greggs down the road.'

Gladstone slurped at his tea like his falsers were about to go swimming. 'Right, Sean, tell us more about this lassie who was found in Edinburgh this morning. We're all ears, aren't we, young Cameron?'

'All ears, sir.'

Bracken thought that Robb looked like a half-shut knife and wondered if he was working long hours.

'She was found in an old, abandoned house that had been picked out by a DIY show for refurbishment. She had a plastic bag round her head. Her legs had been burnt, but not there. There was no indication of a fire. She was tied to the chair by cable ties, but that was only to keep her from toppling off. We got an ID: Claire Thompson. From here in Glenrothes. I'd like to speak to any next of kin.'

Gladstone slurped more of the tea. 'This is good stuff,' he said. 'Go on, show him the photo.'

Robb pulled a clear evidence bag out of his jacket pocket and laid it flat on the table, turning it round for Bracken to see.

Inside was a Polaroid photo. The subject was a woman tied to a chair. She looked exactly like the victim he had seen earlier. There was a plastic bag round her head, hiding her identity, and her legs were on fire. There was no blurred movement, suggesting that she might already be dead at that point.

'Where did you find this?' Bracken asked.

'Show, don't tell,' Gladstone said. 'Isn't that a thing that writers learn?'

'I think so,' Bracken said.

'Then go and show DCI Bracken where you got that,' Gladstone told Robb.

They stood up and Bracken held out a hand. 'Good seeing you again, sir.'

'I have a feeling we'll be keeping in touch on this, Sean. If your victim is indeed this lassie, it looks like she was murdered on our patch, so young Cameron here will be liaising with you good old boys across the water.'

'Ninety-nine per cent chance it's her, I would say.'

'Then let's nail the bastard.'

Bracken and Robb walked out of the canteen and along the corridor.

'He's lost weight, you see that?' Robb said.

'So he was telling me.'

'He had a haircut. The new and improved Benny Gladstone. Well, physically. He still shouts at the top of his voice when something isn't going the way he wants it.'

'He'll have a stroke,' Bracken said as they made their way out into the chill November air.

'Not according to him. His carotid is looking pretty good. No plaque to come bouncing off and go on a trip into his brain. Unlike his old man.'

'He told you about his dad dying of a stroke?' Bracken said.

'No. When he's in a mood, he'll shout, *My dad could do better work than this, and he died of a fucking stroke*. I'm sure it's meant to be an inspirational pep talk. My money's on his ticker giving out first.'

'You got a pool going?'

'Aye. You want in?'

'I do. Put me down for heart attack.'

'Are we a pair of sick bastards or what?' Robb said, grinning, as they got into his car.

'What do you mean "we"? This is all you.'

'Anyway, boss. You always liked going to St Andrews for a day, didn't you? With...what's her name again?'

'Jeanette. Water under the bridge.'

'She was a good laugh.' Robb pulled out onto the main road and headed northeast.

The drive was around twenty miles, and they covered it in half an hour after being stuck behind a bus for a while. They went through Pitscottie, which was a collection of houses and a tea room on the main road to Craigtoun Asylum.

'The land and the hospital were sold off years ago. There's a new country club on the land, but they're still waiting to develop the hospital,' Robb explained. He drove onto a dirt road and stopped behind a couple of vans and a patrol car.

'Forensics are still working inside,' he said as they got out of the car.

'Who found the body?' Bracken asked.

'Two patrol officers. There was a treble-nine call saying somebody was creeping about here. There've been vandals in here recently, as well as YouTubers filming. The country club committee are worried some bastard will set this place on fire before they can develop it.'

'What's stopping them? The committee, I mean.'

'The council or something.'

'What? Somebody not getting their palm greased enough?'

'That's very cynical, boss.'

'Aye, well, I'm a bit older than you, son.' Bracken nodded to part of the security fence that was lying on its face. 'What happened there?'

'Jackie Stewart came belting in and didn't see it. He rearranged it with the front of the patrol car.'

'Christ. That's going to come out of his wages, I hope.'

'He's a big bastard. Mental, so I've heard. Word is, he was flying along here to give an intruder a good hiding.'

'Jesus. That's all we need, some hotshot.'

They walked past the downed fence and round the circular driveway to the main entrance. There was a uniform there, looking thoroughly miserable. He nodded to them as they walked past him into the smelly entrance hall.

'Table for two?' a woman said, grinning at them. She was in her white forensics suit.

'Just show us the way to the bar, if you don't mind,' Robb answered.

'As you wish. There's a wait, though; maybe come back in five years.'

Robb laughed. 'Lynn Shaw, this is DCI Sean Bracken from Edinburgh. He used to be one of us.'

'Then I went to the dark side, apparently,' Bracken said, nodding to the young woman.

'Edinburgh,' she said matter-of-factly.

Bracken raised his eyebrows. 'Could have been Glasgow.'

'Cameron already told me you'd found a victim in Edinburgh. That's why you're here.'

'You take all the mystery out of it,' he said to Robb. 'If you see what I mean.'

Lynn laughed. 'You'll be wanting the tour?' she said.

'Is there a gift shop at the end?' Bracken said.

'Trust me, there's nothing here you'd want. You'd be lucky not to get typhoid, it's that manky. But this is the area where the chair was found, and it's still in place. We've taken so many photos of it from every conceivable angle.'

'That chair will end up in a museum somewhere,' Robb said.

'Or eBay,' Lynn added. 'Maybe Facebook Market-place. Some ghoul will want to plant his arse on it. Maybe keep it in pride of place in his living room. I can imagine the scenario. "Yes, Farquar, this is *the* chair that the young woman was murdered on. What? Of course it's not been washed. Bloody imbecile."'

'There's money in this sort of crap,' Robb said, and Bracken caught a look that passed between them.

'There's no explaining the world,' Lynn said. 'But anyway, it looks like she was brought in here, tied to the chair and set on fire with an accelerant. Not petrol. Not enough damage for that. More like lighter fluid. It wasn't meant to kill, just maim. There are remnants of the fire here. Pieces of clothing and burnt flesh. Whoever did this took a photo, then took her corpse out to a waiting vehicle.'

'Can you tell how long this detritus has been here?' Bracken asked.

'Not long. I can't tell for sure right now, but it looks fresh. Maybe for the last couple of days, no longer than that.'

'How about tyre tracks?'

'Nothing in front because there's the fence. We

surmise he parked round the side and took her that way.'

Bracken looked at Robb. 'That fence panel was lying flat when we parked.'

'Yeah, that was the constable who was driving. Seems he approached a little too fast. Gladstone chewed him a new arsehole. It's one of the St Andrew's crowd, but Gladstone's arms reach far and wide.'

'Has it been dry here?' Bracken asked Lynn.

'Yes. It's been frosty but not enough to make the driveway muddy or anything. There are old tyre tracks, but we'll take an impression anyway. Look around this place, though. There's so much rubbish lying about and half of Fife have trampled through here, not to mention outsiders who've travelled to gawk at the place and film it for YouTube.'

'Any CCTV from the country club next door?' Bracken asked Robb.

'I have somebody over there checking it out.'

'Let me know what the outcome of that is.'

'Of course,' Robb said.

'Nice meeting you, Lynn.'

'You too, Sean. Come back soon.' She smiled at him.

'I'm never far away.'

They walked out into the cold again.

'The photo was just sitting there on the chair?' Bracken said.

'Yes. The sergeant took a photo on his phone, then called it in. When he saw what it was a photo of, they called us in.'

'Somebody wanted us to know where the victim started her journey.'

'They certainly did.'

'Come on, Cameron, let's go and break the news to her family.'

TEN

'How long you been seeing her?' Bracken asked as Robb drove past the country club.

'What do you mean?'

'It's a simple question, pal. How long have you and Miss Lynn been an item?'

Robb made a scoffing sound. 'I don't know what you mean, boss.'

'Of course you bloody well do. Her face lit up like a Christmas tree when you walked in.' Bracken looked out through the windscreen for a second. 'Unless it was me.'

'No disrespect, but I think it was me.'

'I've still got it, son.'

'Not saying you haven't, but you were right: we've been going out for a couple of months.'

'There, that wasn't so hard, was it? I'd still like to think her smile was partly because of me.'

'I think it was. She was thinking, *Thank God I'm going out with the younger one.*'

'Cheeky bastard. Some things certainly don't change.'

Robb grinned.

Twenty minutes later, they were pulling up to a detached bungalow on the north side of Glenrothes. They got out and walked up to the door, and Bracken rapped on the letterbox.

He looked around while they waited to see if anybody was at home. It was a nice neighbourhood, but these days a nice neighbourhood could be quantified by the lack of graffiti on the side of a house.

Nobody answered.

Bracken turned to Robb. 'Can you call back later and give the family the death message?'

'Of course. I'll call you afterwards. Maybe they're out looking for her. The mother reported Claire missing and she was frantic.'

Bracken couldn't imagine his Sarah being missing and driving himself mental waiting for the knock on the door.

'Right, let's not give the neighbours a show.'

They got back in the car and Robb's phone rang.

He spoke briefly to the caller before hanging up. 'Gladstone wants to see you before you go.'

'Let's not keep the man waiting then.'

Gladstone was waiting in the incident room for them when they got back. He was sitting at a table by himself with photos spread out on it. They were face down, except one. Other detectives were busy at computers and one was working on a whiteboard.

'Tea?' Gladstone asked.

'I'm fine, sir, thanks,' Bracken said. 'I don't want to get halfway across the Queensferry Crossing and have to stop for a pish.'

Gladstone laughed. 'Not good. Especially if it's windy. But pull up a chair, both of you. You're making the fucking room look untidy.'

Bracken and Rob each pulled over an office chair and sat either side of the older man.

'What do you see here?' Gladstone asked Bracken after he turned a photo over.

Bracken looked at it. It showed the corpse of a woman sitting in a wheelchair, her legs burnt. Her head was wrapped in a plastic bag, taped round her neck.

'I know this looks like our victim, but I don't understand,' Robb said.

'You will, Cam, son, you will,' Gladstone said. 'This

is Rita Solomon. The crime scene is another old room in Craigtoun. This was the original victim from thirty years ago. A local teenager was found standing over her body. Jerome Kelly. He was special needs. He didn't admit to killing her, but he was locked away in an asylum. Strathmore. A year later, he was brought back to Craigtoun because it too had been turned into an asylum and the smaller place in Kirkcaldy was closed down after a year.'

'How long was he in there for?' Robb asked.

'Ten years, give or take.' Gladstone turned back to Bracken, then turned over another photo he'd been keeping face down. 'You should recognise this place.'

Bracken did. Sort of. 'I could tell you, but I'd have to kill you afterwards.'

'Ya daft bastard,' Gladstone said. 'It's Writers' Court in Edinburgh. You go through the vennel from the High Street, then down a few steps is a flat area before the steps leading down to Warriston Close, and they continue down to Cockburn Street. I thought this case today was familiar.'

'I'm not following, sir,' Robb said.

'This was a case from twenty years ago, ten years after the original murder. Diane Chisolm was abducted and murdered. We think her murderer killed her first, then took her to the scene in a van or something. He wheeled her down there, wrapped her face in a plastic bag, then set fire to her.'

'Did you ever get anybody for it?' Bracken asked.

'Naw. We had a suspect. Guess who? Jerome Kelly.'

'When you ask people to guess, you've got to give them a second,' Bracken complained.

'Were you going to say Jerome Kelly?'

'I was actually.'

'Lyin' bastard. Anyway, Kelly had been in Craigtoun and he'd developed an unhealthy obsession with a nurse, so they shipped him out to Gogarburn. Then he was released into the care of the community because they closed that hospital. He was put into the Royal Edinburgh, to help him adjust to the outside world. Which meant he was allowed out on his own for periods of time. And he went out and committed that murder. We were sure of it. I was working in Edinburgh at the time, but we could never pin it on him. And guess what?'

Bracken looked at Gladstone, wondering where the man was going with this. Robb looked down at the photos.

'He really did kill Rita, the first victim,' Robb said.

'If only, son. We could have had him locked up for good this time, but no, that's not where I was going. Sean?'

'He attacked a man in a supermarket one Saturday afternoon.'

'That's not guessing, that's cheating, ya bastard. You looked it up.' Gladstone shook his head.

'I was one of the uniforms who turned up that day when we got the shout. It was just before I joined CID.'

'You'll know what he was like then, this Kelly.'

'Scruffy, scrawny wee bastard he was, if I remember correctly,' Bracken said. 'Gave the security guards in the shopping centre some guff. They caught him trying to get onto a bus after he'd got his arse kicked by a bloke he attacked in a supermarket.'

Gladstone nodded in agreement. 'Aye. Long story short, he got a talking-to. Not prosecuted, mind. Oh no, that would have been too fucking easy. Because he was daft, he was given a stern talking-to and told to behave himself. But we had cause to talk to him after the fight And got nowhere. The bloke he attacked was a guy called Ray Chisolm. Diane Chisolm was his wife. She was a nurse at the Royal Edinburgh and Kelly recognised her in the supermarket, he said. She didn't work his ward, but he admitted to liking her.'

'Seems to me he wasn't that daft,' Robb said.

'I would agree with you there, son,' Gladstone said. 'But there's no proof he murdered her. There were no witnesses. Kelly was in the Royal Ed at the time, apparently, but that basically meant fuck all. The nursing staff was down to a bare minimum and they freely admitted the patients who were being released had the run of the place. They were supervised, but they weren't monitored like they had been when they were in Gogarburn. They knew the patients were about to be released anyway, so nobody gave a shit. Diane's killer was never found.'

'In theory, this guy Kelly could have walked out of the Royal Edinburgh, killed this nurse and then gone back again,' Bracken said.

'It looked that way, but by then nobody gave a toss. Now, here's something else you need to know: Kelly had daily contact with a psychologist. Know who it was he was seeing?'

Both of the other men shook their head.

'Ailsa Connolly.' Gladstone turned to Bracken. 'Your friend. If anybody got inside that bastard's head, it was her.'

Ailsa Connolly had spent time in the Royal Edinburgh, not just as a psychologist but as a patient after she was convicted of killing six men.

'She's out on release now, under licence,' Bracken said.

'So I heard. She's a Church of Scotland minister now, isn't she?' Gladstone said.

'She is.'

'You should go and talk to her, son. Get the skinny on that daft bastard.'

'I don't think she'll be able to give me any details about him. Patient confidentiality and all that.'

'She doesn't have to give you secrets, just an opinion.'

'Maybe I'll do that,' Bracken said. He tapped one of the photos. 'Is our latest victim related in any way to the victim from twenty years ago?'

'We're still looking into that, but nothing so far.'

Bracken looked at his watch. It had been a long day. But he still had one more thing to do before calling it a day.

'I'll call ahead and talk to Ailsa Connolly tomorrow,' Bracken said.

'What if she doesn't want to talk to you, sir?' Robb asked.

Gladstone looked at him. 'She has no choice. Anyone of detective inspector rank and above can go and speak to her any time he or she likes. It's part of Connolly's licence. Even if she doesn't want to, she can go and fucking whistle. Or else she'll be back in the secure unit before she can belt out the first chorus of "She'll Be Coming Round the Mountain".'

'I'm sure it won't be a problem for her,' Bracken said.

'I've already done a search on Jerome Kelly. He's still kicking around, over on your side of the water still, Sean. And believe it or not, he's had a warning from us.

The polis. For touching a wee lassie on a bus.' Gladstone shook his head. 'I'd touch the fucker with the toe of my boot, let me tell you. Go and have a word with him. And keep me in the loop on this, Sean. Whenever somebody is available at Claire Thompson's house, I'll go round with Cameron here. Then I'll call you.'

'Catch you later,' Bracken said, then he walked out with Robb.

'You think this Kelly guy is our man?' Robb said.

'When has anything been this easy, Cameron?'

'I don't remember it ever being this easy.'

They walked out into the cold air as darkness was coming down. 'I'll give you a call tomorrow, see where we're at,' Bracken said.

'Take care, sir.'

Bracken drove off, wondering why Jerome Kelly would come back to Fife to murder a woman, and why now?

He had plenty of time to think about it. But first, he had to go and see a man about a dog.

ELEVEN

'She's not coming,' Ed Bracken said, looking at his watch again.

'She told you she'd be here,' Bob Long said. 'Give the lassie time.'

Ed looked at his friend as they stood outside the domestic arrivals hall at Edinburgh airport.

'Do you think I'm a stupid old fart?' he asked.

'Of course not. You deserve love, Ed. You had a good marriage, but your wife has been gone for a long time. You deserve to move on.'

Ed was holding a small bunch of flowers that they'd picked up at a petrol station.

'She's twenty years younger than me. I keep thinking I'm a stupid old man at times.'

People were rushing towards them like a flash flood and skirting round them, a sea of faces, but Ed was focused on seeing just one.

'Nonsense. You know there's somebody for every-body,' Bob said.

'Don't make it sound like I'm a bloody hunchback.'

Ed's mobile phone dinged and he took it out of his pocket and looked at the screen. 'Oh, crap.' He looked at Bob. 'She's not coming.'

'She'll be here, mate. You watch.'

'No, I mean she's not coming. She just sent me a text. She couldn't make the flight. Her brother, Joe, took ill again and he's been hospitalised.'

'Oh, God, that's too bad. Poorly, is he?'

'He's got some sort of illness. He's been in and out of hospital all his life.'

Another ding, another message.

'She said the airline won't refund her money, so she'll have to buy another ticket.'

'That's a costly game for her. It must cost her a fortune.'

Ed looked at his friend. 'It costs me a fortune.'

'What do you mean?'

'She can't afford this on her own. I help her by sending her money.'

Bob didn't say anything for a moment. 'You know what you're doing, I suppose.'

'She's had a hard life, mate. What with their parents dying when they were young. Then her brother got that disease. She says she's lucky to have me and she's looking forward to coming up here to live once she gets a carer sorted out for her brother.'

Bob turned to start walking back to the multi-storey car park. 'What does he have? Her brother. If you don't mind me asking.'

'It's some long name. She told me, but I can't remember. Lymphatic something or other.'

'That's a shame. Poor bugger.'

Another text.

'She says she'll try and get up next weekend. Meantime, I'll send her some money out of my savings. For another plane ticket.' Ed looked at Bob. 'I told her she could stay at the guest house since you have a couple of rooms free and I would pay for it, and she says she's grateful for that.'

Ed looked despondent.

'Never mind, pal,' Bob said, putting an arm around his friend. 'Hopefully, it won't be long before she comes up.' But Bob knew in his heart that Elizabeth would never be up from London.

TWELVE

The cold had turned the rain to snow on the way down from Fife back to Edinburgh. Bracken thought about calling Chaz but held back. Doing so would make him feel that he couldn't go anywhere without checking in with her first.

Is that what it really is, Bracken? he asked himself. Maybe the truth was closer to the fact that the wee short-arse was about to ask Bracken's ex-wife to marry him. He had always thought that Catherine deserved somebody in her life, and he had wished her well when she was dating, but the thought that this little man, Leon, would want to take her down the aisle irritated him for some reason, and it wasn't jealousy.

That's why he was going to make a detour on his way home.

The traffic was heaving going the other way,

leaving the capital, but Edinburgh-bound it was still busy enough. The cars shot past him on the new bridge, going too fast, too close, as usual, despite the snow making the road slicker now. He kept the car at a slower pace, because the last thing he wanted right now was to be in a car accident.

He took the slip road for South Queensferry and connected down through Kirkliston, so he could head along past Ingliston. Then he had to head through Corstorphine.

A song came on the radio, one of Chaz's favourites. He listened to the words as he thought about her. He couldn't hope to find somebody better than her. She was funny, good to be with and wanted to move their relationship to the next level: living together. Would they get married some day? That he didn't have the answer to. Some people lived with each other all their lives without getting married and were quite happy. Somehow, he didn't see Chaz being happy with that, despite being a divorcee. Her ex-husband had cheated on her, but she had dusted herself down and now she was ready to move on. He didn't want to be the second man who had disappointed her in her life.

Eventually, he reached the South Bridge and turned into Drummond Street, where he managed to find a parking space. He walked back to the main road and stood looking over at his destination. The Festival

Theatre. The huge, glass-fronted edifice looked good in the drifting snow, lit up from behind like a Christmas tree.

He decided to play a game of chicken with the traffic and ran across the road, only to narrowly avoid being creamed by a bicyclist, who told Bracken he thought the detective might possibly be into self-abuse. Bracken felt it might be a good idea to release the day's frustrations on the man's bike helmet should he decide that Bracken was a moron who needed to be taught a lesson and that he, the cyclist, was the very one to be teaching that lesson.

Bracken stopped and stared at the man, but he merely cycled away, collecting snowflakes in his beard.

Bracken walked through the entrance and found a member of staff.

'I'd like to speak to the manager,' he said, showing his warrant card.

The young man nodded and scuttled off to find somebody. Bracken was admiring the place when somebody behind him cleared their throat.

He turned round and saw a woman dressed in a skirt and jacket looking at him. She was young but exuded authority.

'I'm looking for the manager,' he said, showing his warrant card again.

'Then you've found her. Amanda Craig. And what can I do for you?'

He stood looking at her, not because she was a woman in charge but because she didn't look anything like Leon.

'I was actually looking for Leon Harris,' he said.

'Unless that's the name of a play we're putting on, you're flat out of luck,' she said, a smile playing on her lips.

Great. A bloody comedian.

'As much as I'm sure a play would be very entertaining, unfortunately this particular Leon Harris is very real.'

'You think that somebody called Leon Harris is the manager here?' she said.

'I was led to believe that was the case.'

People were starting to come in and Amanda led Bracken over to one side. 'I'm not sure who told you that, but there's nobody called Leon here. The previous manager was called Dick, and he hasn't worked here in a long time. Real obnoxious so-and-so he was. Dick by name and all that.'

'Nobody on the payroll called Leon? Not even the janny?'

'Not even the cleaning crew, no.'

Bracken looked at her for a moment as if she was about to burst out laughing, slap him on the arm and say to him, *'Should have seen your face.'* But none of that happened.

'Are you sure you're in the right theatre?' Amanda asked.

'Yes.' Although he was starting to feel like the previous manager and thought he might change his name to Dick. 'I'll call my contact and see if she made a mistake. Maybe she was misinformed.'

'Are you sure it's nothing I can help you with?' Amanda asked. Her smile was wider now and her eyes were bright, as if she was about to burst out laughing. *Remember that Dick who used to work here? I just had his brother in earlier. Two peas in a pod they were, only this one was carrying a wee badge thing.*

Feeling like he had just found the warrant card in a lucky bag, he smiled back at her, one professional to another. *'Fucking public,'* he hoped his smile conveyed, but he suspected it made him look like a deviant. All he needed was the thick glasses and a glaikit look and he'd have the whole set.

'That's all. I'll make a phone call.' *A fucking bomb threat; see how you like that.*

'Well, if there's anything else I can help you with, be sure to call me.' She turned and walked away, making him feel like she had just dumped him on their first date. Birly-baws, the unluckiest bastard in the world, had just got kicked into touch. Again.

People were looking at him like he was something a dog had puked up on the carpet.

'He dies at the end,' he said, walking out, forgetting that he wasn't at the pictures but at a theatre and they were here to see a play and not a film.

He took his phone out. The snow had stopped coming down, now that it had left the pavements slick.

'Catherine? It's me,' he said, hoping she could hear him over the wind.

'*Who is this? Filthy pervert. I'm calling the police.*'

'That material's not new, I'll have you know.'

His ex laughed on the other end. '*What's up, Sean?*'

'You told me that Leon was the manager at the Festival Theatre, right?'

'*I did.*'

'Is he still the manager there?'

'*Yes. Why?*'

'I was going to see if he could get me some free tickets for the Christmas panto this year, that's all.'

'*I'll ask him.*'

'That would be great. Thanks.'

'*Do you want to come round and pick up your laundry from this morning, or shall I just put it in my drawer for next time?*'

Next time. He promised himself that he wouldn't

get himself into that situation again, but he knew there would be a next time.

'I'm sure Widow Twankey can decide.'

'Drawer it is then.'

'Are you seeing Leon tonight?'

'You are *keen to see the panto, aren't you?'*

'Just wondering, that's all.'

'No. He's working. He'll be there now.'

What? Washing glasses on the side? Maybe he's the window cleaner. Or maybe a busker outside. Whatever it is, he isn't the fucking manager.

'Thanks, Catherine. Maybe you could tell him I'll pop in one night to pick up the tickets.' That should make the bastard sweat a bit.

'I will.'

He disconnected the call before crossing the road, being especially careful to avoid any cyclists. He got back to the car and sat with the heater on for a moment, pointing it in the direction of the windscreen. Then he dialled Ed's number, wanting to talk to the old man before he saw him in person.

'Ed's office, Ed speaking. How may I help you?'

'That's wearing thin.'

'I'm sorry, but I'm very happy with my mobile phone carrier, I already have a warranty for my car, and no, you can't have my bank account details.'

'Can I ask the question I was going to ask before I forget why I called in the first place?'

'Do you know your party's extension?'

Fuck's sake. 'I do have an extension, and it's called a baton. How about I show you next time I see you and ram it –'

'That's not very nice, coming from somebody who wants a secret kept.'

'Dad, I do *not* want a secret kept.'

'Really now? Chaz is here. Will I pass you over to her?'

'You're enjoying this, aren't you?'

'I get no such enjoyment out of this filth. If you would learn to keep it in your pants, I wouldn't be a party to this.'

Bracken hoped Chaz wasn't standing within earshot of the old man. Max barked in the background.

'Listen, you like Catherine, don't you?'

'Of course I do.'

'Then let's not cause trouble for her. She needed my advice on something, and I got carried away with the booze.'

Ed laughed. *'I know that, ya daft bugger. I'm just winding you up. But maybe you could remind me of what happened when you take me to the pub one night. Be aware, though: I might forget to put my hand in my pocket.'*

'Nothing new then.'

'I heard that.'

'You were meant to. You know that blackmailing a police officer is punishable by a kick in the bollocks?'

'Listen, son, if anything happens to me, my pal has instructions to post the letters. The ones describing just who they should be looking at in connection with the case. But to be honest, I don't think they'll be looking far, do you?'

'I only threatened you with a kick in the bollocks, not putting you through a wood-chipper. But anyway, we've gone off on a tangent. Please remember what I said.'

'About what?'

'I'm putting you in a home. Just remember this conversation when you have to sit and watch a Punch and Judy show every night before they give you the sleepy meds. I'll be home in a wee while.'

He hung up just as Ed started to defame the famous pair of puppets and was telling his son where the puppet master could insert the deadly duo.

He went round the block along the one-way system, wondering just where the hell Leon Harris actually was. He was about to head back to the guest house when he took a different turn and headed down to Leith again. He was visiting here more than a whore's best customer, but such was life.

He parked in the street outside Catherine's block of flats on double yellow lines and put the police sign on the dash. He walked down through the bollards to Commercial Street. What had once been bonded warehouses was now upmarket restaurants where a meal would cost Bracken a day's pay. He crossed the road, careful not to slide on the snow and fall on his arse in case he was mowed down by an enthusiastic bus driver.

Over on his right was the old Leith Custom House, a Gothic-looking building that wouldn't have even made it on an unimaginative architect's drawing board nowadays. On the left was the street he was looking for: Sandport. He walked down and through a private entranceway to the houses at the back.

He stood outside the stairway door with the electronic buzzers. He saw the number but didn't see the name he was looking for. He pressed the number and a woman's voice answered.

'Police. Can I have a word?' he said.

There was hesitation before a woman answered, 'Of course.' She buzzed him in and he climbed the two flights of stairs, the snow slipping off his short-cut hair and jacket.

The woman was waiting for him when he got there. He could have been an axe murderer and he wouldn't have had to break sweat to gain entry to kill her, but he brought out nothing more dangerous than his warrant card.

'I'm DCI Sean Bracken. I'm looking for Leon Harris.'

He studied her face. She looked nondescript, somebody you would walk past in the street, but on closer inspection he saw a small scar on the left side of her mouth. Her dark hair was pulled back into a ponytail and she was dressed for comfort in a baggy sweatshirt and jogging bottoms.

She looked puzzled. 'There's nobody by that name lives here,' she said.

'He's a short man, maybe five-six, with short hair and glasses,' he said, in case she was mistaken, but surely she would know if a man lived in the house or not.

'Sorry. I live alone. I don't even recognise the description,' she said, wrapping her arms around herself as if all the heat in the flat was making a run for it.

For just a split second, Bracken doubted himself. He was sure this was the address Catherine had given him, but there was a little nagging doubt now.

'Sorry to have bothered you.'

'No problem,' she said, stepping back and closing the door on him. He went back outside and thought about calling Catherine, but decided he would just go up and see her instead.

It was a two-minute walk, unless you were trying not to slip on heavy snow and break a hip. He trudged back up the road, head down, hunching into his overcoat. He was running several scenarios through his head, with Leon front and centre, and none of them ended well for the small man.

Not the manager of the Festival Theatre. Didn't live where Catherine said he did. What was the little bastard up to?

THIRTEEN

'Did he say if he's on his way home for dinner?' Chaz Cullen asked Ed.

'I don't know, to be honest. He's working that new case you were at.'

'The girl with the burnt legs. Sounds like the title of a novel.'

'I tell you, I'm glad I was in banking and not looking at corpses every day like you.'

They were sitting on the couch in the guest living room, watching TV. Max was sitting next to Chaz as she scratched his ear.

'Listen, Ed, I'm going to go home and make dinner. When Sean comes in, tell him he can pop over for a bite to eat. I already mentioned it to him today.' Chaz got up and smiled at the older man. Max stood up too, wondering if it was time to play with the ball.

'Okay, I'll tell him.'

'You never told me where your friend is staying,' Chaz said.

'She couldn't make it. Her brother got sick.'

'Shame. That's both of us disappointed today. Take care, Ed.' She petted Max one more time and the dog watched her leave.

Chaz left the guest house. Ed hoped his son wasn't messing the lassie about. Then he got a text on his phone.

I made it after all! I was able to transfer my ticket at the last minute and now I'm here!!

Ed's first reaction was to replicate having a heart attack; the second was to barely hold on to his bladder – neither fact would he share with Elizabeth.

Terrific! he wrote back. *Where are you?*

I called a friend of mine in Edinburgh. You remember the one I told you about? She's letting me stay with her. I didn't want you spending money on me, my love.

Well, too fucking late for that, he thought. But he chastised himself. Elizabeth needed him now. What she *didn't* need was for him to get sarky. She'd had enough abuse from her ex-husband without Ed adding to it.

'You wanting dinner now, Ed?' Bob Long said,

coming into the room. Ed could add *nearly shitting himself* to the list of reactions.

'I'm not hungry, Bob, thanks.'

'Get away. Who are you and what have you done with the real Ed Bracken?'

'Seriously. I just got a text from Elizabeth. She's in Edinburgh!'

'How the hell did she manage that?'

'It's a long story, but she told her friend about coming and she's letting Elizabeth stay at her place in Leith.'

'Why didn't she tell you about this friend before?'

'She did. I just forgot.'

'Okay then. Are you going to see her?'

They both looked out of the bay window at the snow coming down.

'Of course I am, silly bugger,' Ed said, standing up and beaming a smile at his friend. 'Maybe we can go for a drink.'

'Just be careful.'

'I will, Bob. I've been round the block a few times.'

'I meant, don't fall and break a hip.'

'I'm more worried about the bus getting stuck and me needing a piss.'

'You should try those adult nappies.'

'Recommend them, do you?' Ed said, grinning.

'Aye, well, after falling through the ceiling of a

burning house and breaking my back, the nerves are out of sync and I need a piss more often than usual.'

Ed's face fell. 'Oh, I'm sorry, pal. I forgot.'

Bob laughed. 'Just pulling your ding-dong.'

'What are these emoji things again? *SMH. Shaking my head.*'

'*Rolling on the floor laughing my arse off.* That's what Mary sends to me. But seriously, take it easy out there, pal. It's getting slick.'

'I will. I'll just take the boy here for a piss and then put him in my room.'

'Nonsense. He can stay with us. You'll probably be late, getting your end away.'

'Here, I get enough of that from the heir. I don't need you sticking it to me.'

Bob laughed. 'Get Max settled, then we'll put him through in my living room.'

'Cheers, Bob.'

Twenty minutes later, Ed had settled the dog and had put on his thick winter jacket and stuck a beanie hat on. Then he left to catch a bus.

FOURTEEN

'I think you drank me dry last night,' Catherine Bracken said, taking her ex-husband's overcoat and hanging it on a hook in the hallway closet. 'The fridge is devoid of tinnies.'

'I'll settle for a cup of coffee,' Bracken said, following her through to the living room. 'Is Sarah in?'

'She's staying at her friend's house again.' She paused. 'Have you eaten?'

'No, I haven't been home.'

'What's Chaz going to say about that?'

'We're not joined at the hip, Cath.'

'I know that, but she *is* your girlfriend. You should communicate with her.'

'We made it a rule not to see each other every night. To give each other space,' he said, sitting down on the couch that he had woken up on that morning.

'That doesn't mean you can't call her.'

'I'm not even finished work yet.'

'Really? What are you working on at this time of the evening?'

'You for one should know how crazy my hours get.'

'I also know how much you can spin a tale, Bracken.'

'That kettle won't boil itself,' he said in reply.

She stood looking at him.

'Oh, right, I'll go and put it on,' he said, getting up. She followed him into the kitchen.

Bracken didn't want to come right out and ask Catherine for Leon's address, thinking he would make some more enquiries first.

'Have you managed to talk to Leon about the theatre tickets?' Bracken asked.

'No, not yet.'

'And you're sure he'll be able to get them?'

She turned away from him and left the kitchen. He made two mugs of coffee and took them through. Catherine was sitting in a chair, chewing on a nail. She smiled as she took her mug. She took a sip and set it down on a side table next to her.

'Is everything okay with you and Chaz, Sean?'

'Of course it is,' he said.

'Then why are you here with me and not at home with her?'

'I just got to thinking after you told me about Leon's impending proposal. Are you sure you don't want to get hitched?'

'Do any of us?'

'Don't be coy.'

'I just said that I think he might be heading down that road. He told me he loves me and he's willing to wait until our wedding night to...you know...'

Fuck my ex-wife. 'I know.'

'I'm just hesitant.'

'Would you live here?' he asked. 'You know...after the wedding.'

'Leon wants to. He just rents his place. He says he could move in here until we find a place together. He would put money down, but his ex-wife cleaned him out in the divorce. But as I said last night, I don't want to marry him. He's moving things along too fast. I don't want him spending the night, never mind spending the rest of his life with me.'

Bracken nodded. 'You have to tell him. End it now, if you have to.'

'I can't. Not at this moment in time. I know what you're thinking: Leon's trying it on. But he's not. He said he got cleaned out, but she still has to give him half the money from the sale of their house. He's living on his wages just now, but he'll have a few notes when the house gets sold.'

Bracken knew without asking that Catherine had given him money. He'd seen it before with victims of financial crime.

'Where did he live?' *Where the fuck does he live now?*

'Cramond. He's expecting a fair penny. You can see it online.' She told him the address and he mentally filed it away.

Nothing was making sense to Bracken. 'Who is he staying with just now?'

'His sister. That's his sister's house round in Sandport.'

He nodded and drank his coffee. Why would his sister say Leon didn't stay there? Or that she had never heard of him?

He would think about it in the morning.

'Want to watch some TV? I can call for a pizza.'

'Great. I'd like that.'

FIFTEEN

Ed took a black cab down to the Shore. It was better being mugged by the driver's meter than a skinhead with a knife. At least he'd still have his bank card when he got out of the taxi.

'Be careful out there, pal. Roads are getting icy.'

'Aye, thanks, pal,' Ed answered, but he wasn't really paying attention. His heart was hammering again; not a good thing for a man in his late sixties, but he also felt a sense of excitement he hadn't felt since he had been married. His wife, Sean's mum, was long gone now, and he had to admit that although he loved his dog, lying next to a German shepherd in bed wasn't cutting it.

He went into the pub across from the ship that was permanently docked on the Water of Leith as a floating restaurant. He was surprised how busy the pub was.

The sound of laughter greeted him, as did the warmth. The snow was coming down heavily now and he was dripping onto the floor. He made his way to the bar and eventually caught the attention of the barman.

Elizabeth wasn't here. He could feel it. *Jesus*. He looked at his old watch and saw he was ten minutes early, so he decided not to panic.

'And you must the Amazing Ed you keep telling me about,' a female's voice said from behind.

He put his pint down, smiled and turned. 'Elizabeth?' Of course it was Elizabeth; otherwise the hoors were getting prettier.

'Oh, Ed! I'm so glad you could come down.'

He was speechless for a moment before a wee cog in his brain managed to turn and operate his tongue again. 'Drink?'

She nodded. 'G and T, please. Let me get it.'

'Och, away. I'll get it.'

Once again he tried to get the barman to look over in his direction. If the baw-bag had more than two brain cells, he'd be dangerous. Eventually, Ed got served and he kept his newly working tongue in check. He just smiled, thanked the man and silently told him he was a useless part of a female's anatomy.

'There you go,' he said as they squeezed their way through to the back, where Elizabeth thought she could see somebody leaving. She was correct and they snagged the table before a pair of fat bastards could get it, unable to squeeze through the throng as niftily as Ed.

'I can't believe you're here,' Ed said.

'Me neither.'

'I mean, how did you get here? When you said your brother was ill, I thought my chances of meeting you were nil.'

'It wasn't as serious as I first thought. So I called the airline and they switched my tickets.'

'That's fantastic.'

Ed had seen photos of Elizabeth on a chat site and they'd started talking after he'd posted a photo of Max. When she told him that she was a dog lover but didn't have a dog at the moment, they'd got chatting. Then she'd told him about her brother and how ill he was.

Elizabeth reached across for his hand. 'I appreciate how you've helped me, Ed. I couldn't have gone through this without you. Leaving my job was the hardest thing I've ever had to do. I loved being a nurse. When my brother gets a full-time nurse sorted, I can think about going back to work. I even thought about getting a job up here, if you'd like me to stay.'

'Of course I would.'

She smiled at him and took her hand back.

Ed drank some of his pint and thought about how he would break the news to her that he didn't have his own place yet, that he was working on it. He hadn't lied to her, merely left out that fine detail.

'You're going to be staying with your friend for a while?' he asked, hoping his puss wasn't going red.

'Just till we get our own place, Ed. Then I can have my little boy come and live with me.'

'Beg pardon?' he said, almost dropping his glass onto the table.

'Didn't I tell you? I have a teenage son. You'll love him.' She smiled at him and got up from the table. He loved her smile, and the little scar coming up from her top lip had a strange attraction for him.

He watched her go to the ladies'. He hadn't been able to believe his luck when a woman twenty years his junior had fallen for him. Now a little alarm bell was going off in his head. A teenage son? Why hadn't she mentioned him? Had the little bastard been in a young offenders' institute? Christ, that was all he needed. There was no way he wanted to be bringing up somebody else's child. Not a teenager. How old was he? Working age? School age?

'You've gone and got yourself into the shitter this time, Eddie old son,' he told himself. Still, it wasn't too late to get out of it. Was it?

Elizabeth was standing looking in the mirror of the ladies' bathroom when the door opened. She was applying lipstick, leaning closer to the glass, when the figure stopped behind her.

'So?' the man said.

She stopped what she was doing and stood up straight. 'Unless you identify as a woman, I wouldn't get caught in here. The punters might not understand and might give you a hiding.'

'Fuck 'em. I asked you a question.'

She turned to face him, then had to look down a bit. 'I told you I was doing fine. It's all going well. Don't fuck it up now.'

'He doesn't suspect anything?'

'No. I told you it would go well. He's in love with me. Just give me a little bit more time. I've almost cleaned him out.'

'Are you taking him back to the flat?'

Elizabeth scoffed at him. 'Of course not. Do you think I'm some kind of tart? Besides, I told him I have a teenage boy. That put the brakes on. He'll think about it now, maybe decide that I'm not the woman for him, but by the time he realises it, I'll have emptied his bank account.'

'Good,' the man said.

'What about you?'

'I've changed phones now. I have the money. All we need now is for you to finish the job and we're off.'

'Have patience.'

'Just another few days?'

'Yes, just another few days. Keep out of sight until then, and don't draw attention to yourself. Like coming into the ladies'.'

'Just keep the old codger happy for a little while longer.'

'What about the copper?' Elizabeth asked.

'He's sticking his nose in now. He'll get it chopped off if he's not careful.'

SIXTEEN

Bracken had had an unsettled night and he felt knackered as he drove along the M90 towards Falkirk. Outside of Stirling, there was a choice of which road to take to Killearn, and he just stuck to the road he was on and took the A811.

He'd called ahead and been told it was okay for him to drop in any time. Of course it was: as Gladstone, his old boss, had said, this was part of Ailsa Connolly's licence. It wasn't every serial killer who got to walk out of a psychiatric unit.

It took him an hour and a half, which he thought was lucky since the roads were like a skating rink in places. The village was covered in snow, but the main road had been taken care of. He had been told that the assistant minister wasn't on duty that day, so he needed to make the trip to her house. She lived on a little private road with maybe three or four houses that Bracken could see. This road wasn't as well ploughed as the main road had been, but he managed to get up with a little bit of swearing and a prayer.

Ailsa Connolly was standing at the front door waiting for him. She was smiling.

'I bet you enjoyed that,' Bracken said, locking the car. 'Watching me come up there like a rally driver.'

'What? I was impressed by how you handled it. If that was Robert, he'd have had the car through the hedge already.'

He shook her hand and she invited him in. They went through to the living room, where a log fire was throwing heat out. It felt good.

'I'll take your jacket. Sit yourself down wherever you like. The kettle's just off the boil.'

'Thanks, Ailsa.'

She turned to look at him, still holding his overcoat. 'It's Anne now. Anne Marshall. Finally, I'm using my married name. Besides, some people might take umbrage at the fact their new assistant minister is a reformed killer.'

She smiled and left the room.

Ailsa had been found not guilty by reason of diminished responsibility and had been sent to the state prison in Carstairs, but had then been transferred to Edinburgh when a new secure wing was built at the back of the Royal Edinburgh psychiatric hospital. She had been the force psychologist at one time, even seeing Bracken as a patient before she was arrested.

She came back in with a tray. Bracken was pleased to see it had a plate of biscuits.

'Robert not here?' he asked her.

'No. He only works part time now down in Edinburgh and so he stays there three days a week. It saves him a lot of driving. We kept the house in Morningside, so he doesn't have to worry about finding a place to stay.'

She put the tray on the coffee table in front of him. He had chosen the couch, seeing papers and a pair of reading glasses sitting on the chair next to the fire.

'I'll let you pour your own milk,' she said, adding her own from the small jug before sitting down. He did the same and took a chocolate digestive.

'How have you been, Sean?' she said. Bracken hadn't given her a heads-up about the case, but it wasn't like this was some backwater that didn't know what the internet was.

'I'm doing fine.'

'Still keeping Chaz hanging on?' Ailsa was in her forties and was somebody Bracken could have seen himself settling down with in another place, another time. Robert Marshall was older, but he and Ailsa made it work. He was a psychologist at the Royal Edinburgh, where he had met Ailsa. Bracken was glad to see she hadn't killed him.

'I wouldn't use the term "hanging on", but we're still seeing each other.' *Barely.*

'Does she have any effects from the trauma she suffered last year? Being held captive by a nutcase who was going to kill her and the others?'

'She did for a while, to be honest, but she seems to have got over it.'

'Is there a future for you, do you think? If you don't mind my asking.'

'I'm taking it one day at a time,' he said, sipping more coffee. The heat was different from the gas fire in the guest house. It seeped into the bones and made him feel like he could take a nap.

Ailsa smiled and nodded. 'You do know I'm a trained psychologist. It was my job to cut through the shit. I think you're running away from your relationship and that it hasn't got much further to go down the line. Who is she?'

'Who's who?'

'The other woman in your life? I think you're conflicted. Knowing you, I don't think you would cheat on Chaz, because your wife cheated on you, hence the reason she's called the ex-wife. But something's holding you back.'

Bracken smiled and held up a hand. 'You're on the wrong track there, Ailsa, but thanks anyway.'

'Am I, Sean? If I had to hazard a guess, I would say it's Catherine. She hurt you way back when, but the catalyst for the breakup wasn't your doing.'

'Can we drop it?'

'Of course we can. Now you're here to talk about Jerome Kelly.'

Bracken felt himself sweating even more now. Ailsa Connolly had an intelligence far above that of anybody else he knew, and that was why she had run rings round him when he was seeing her. He had been sure he could have taken things further with her, but he hadn't pursued it.

'I'm interested in Kelly. What made him tick. When he was released into the care of the community,' Bracken said.

'I can't talk about that. Confidentiality and all that.'

Bracken nodded. 'I understand. I just thought I would ask anyway. The answer's always no if you don't ask. We think he's killed again.'

'Ailsa Connolly can't help you.'

'I know, you just said.'

'If somebody were to ask you where you got the information, then you wouldn't be lying. Ailsa didn't give you any information. But I'm Anne Marshall now.'

A smile crossed Bracken's face. He reached for another digestive. 'I'm all ears.'

'Considering the things I've done in the past, telling you about this man is nothing.' Ailsa looked through the window for a moment, as if Jerome Kelly himself was standing outside. Then she was back in the room, looking at Bracken.

'Personally, I think the man's evil. He was born evil. He was what my mother used to call a slow learner. I don't think he was mentally ill, but he was slow to learn, and this angered him. He told me he would get angry with people when he was growing up and this anger would fester until he lashed out.'

'What was his home life like?'

'You probably want to hear he grew up in a foster home where he was abused, battered and beaten. But that's not the case. He was given a decent life. In fact, his father had money. They didn't live in poverty. They were spoiled.'

'They?'

'Him and his brother. They were about a year apart. Jerome is the younger one.'

'Was the brother still in the picture when Jerome was your patient?'

'He refused to talk about him. He said his brother was dead to him. But Kelly was a good actor.'

'He could fool people?'

'Oh, yes. But you don't want to know what he was like growing up. What you want is an insight into his head. His thoughts. And that's something you won't find on his criminal record.'

'That's what I'm here for. Help in understanding if he could have killed this girl and taken her to Edinburgh.'

Ailsa looked right at him, all signs of a smile now gone. 'What do you mean, taken her to Edinburgh? I heard that she was found on the outskirts. What you said makes it sound like she wasn't killed there.'

'She wasn't. It's not something we've released to the press.'

'Where did he kill her?'

'Craigtoun Asylum in St Andrews.'

Again, Ailsa was quiet for a few moments before speaking. 'That's where he was before he got transferred to Edinburgh. Because he had an unhealthy obsession with a nurse.'

'I know all about that. My former boss in Fife told me about it. Then a nurse was left in a wheelchair in a close off the High Street in Edinburgh and set on fire.'

'Jerome told me it all started at Craigtoun. But he didn't mean when it was an asylum. When he was growing up, Craigtoun was an abandoned mansion. It sat empty for years before the health board took it over. It was where he and his brother would play. They would play with their friends, putting on shows, acting like pirates or gangsters, or playing cops and robbers. That's where I think the split personalities started to come out. They were already there, waiting to come out. He told me he wasn't playing the parts when they were messing about in the house. It was the people inside of him coming out.'

'Jesus. It's why he's been able to fool people all this time?'

'I think so. It's why he thought he could fool the police into thinking he didn't kill Rita. Because the persona they were talking to was the one who *didn't* kill Rita. He was very charming when he wanted to be, because that was one of his personalities. He was deemed unfit for trial and sent to Strathmore,' Ailsa confirmed. 'It was getting overcrowded; that's why they were about to refit Craigtoun as another asylum. The building was sound, not like today. A year later, it was finished, and Kelly was taken back there, this time as a patient. He said it reminded him every day of Rita.'

Bracken looked at her, puzzled for a second. 'Why?'

'Kelly knew her. She was his friend, he said. If he had told the authorities that when he got caught, he would have been treated differently, but he didn't say a word about her. Only to me, he said. Sometimes I'd be talking to him and he would give the appearance that he was a docker, swearing and cursing. Other times he'd be calm and very nice, like this was another personality coming out. You never knew which one was going to appear in the office. He only showed three to me.'

'Were you ever scared of him, Ailsa?' Bracken asked.

'No. I didn't think Kelly could do anything physical to me. I didn't fear him at all, and I think he sensed that. He sized me up from the minute he met me, and he knew deep inside that if he tried to touch me, he would more than meet his match. I was a worthy adversary for him physically, and he knew it. He wasn't a big man, but he was very confident. Not all of his personalities were violent, though. When the soft personality came out, he backed down.'

'That old hospital meant a lot to him.'

'Remember, it wasn't a hospital when he and his friends played there. It was an old house. Not a ruin, just abandoned and in pretty good condition. They went in there to play and he had good memories of being in there. Especially of Rita. She was his best friend, he said. She treated him very well.'

'And he didn't confess to killing her?'

'No. He wouldn't talk about it.'

Bracken drank more coffee, finishing the mug. 'Do

you think his docker personality killed her, then Kelly regressed when the police came?'

'I can't be sure. The docker would act tough, but who knows? He never confessed to killing anybody, although that personality wouldn't appear very often.'

'What would bring him out?' Bracken asked.

'When Kelly was pushed into a corner. He would come and go, seemingly at will.'

'How did Kelly seem when he was told he was going to be released into the care of the community?'

'He was excited about getting out. But he had a fight with a man in a supermarket and that rattled him a little, especially since the man got the better of him. I don't know if the docker came out that day or not, but if he did, he went away and the soft personality came forward.'

'Ray Chisolm. I know about that case. Ray's wife was murdered in almost the same way as the victim you told me about in Craigtoun. In exactly the same way as our victim yesterday.'

'Diane. I knew her. Fortunately for Kelly, an orderly gave him an alibi. He was with Kelly around the time they figured Diane was murdered. And apparently Ray had an alibi as well. He was at home with his kids and his sister-in-law had spent the night sleeping on the couch. They were going on a trip that weekend and the sis was helping get the kids ready. They were going to a caravan and she was going to help with the driving.'

'There was no doubt about Ray's innocence?'

Ailsa laughed. 'When do you lot ever believe the husband? He was given the third degree, but his story held up and he was cleared of any wrongdoing.'

'He was a family man. I thought he was a decent bloke.'

'You met him? That attack was twenty years ago.'

Bracken nodded. 'I was one of the uniforms who turned up at the supermarket. I had to tell Ray that the procurator fiscal would do nothing about Kelly as he was in the care of the community. Ray was angry, and I didn't blame him. Later on, he blamed Kelly for his wife's death.'

'How did Kelly seem that day in the supermarket?'

'Scruffy. Hair all over the place. Scraggy beard. Talking tough and swearing at us.'

'You met the docker. Back then, he would have spoken like a decent human being even if he was scruffy, and then the docker would come out. I was the one who suggested he tidy himself up, and much to my surprise, he did. It suited the normal personality. It sounded strange when the docker would come out in him, though. I was hoping that if he altered his appearance, he would stay more with the normal personality, but of course it doesn't work that way. At least he didn't look as scary as he had with his unkempt hair and beard.'

'Now we have a problem then,' Bracken said. 'Two murders twenty years apart and it could be two killers. And you think Kelly didn't kill Rita?'

'I can't be certain. Looking from a policeman's point of view, I would say yes. But from a psychologist's point of view, I would say no. He described loving Rita. And I think the docker left a long time ago.'

'Somebody killed her,' said Bracken, 'and I think it's connected to this new murder somehow. It has to be. Even if it's a copycat, it's still a connection. It's too much of a coincidence for it not to be.'

'Obviously, I haven't seen Kelly in the last eight years or so, since I was incarcerated,' said Ailsa, 'but Robert took over. He can't tell you anything, because he's still a practising psychologist, but what I can tell you is this: Jerome Kelly was moving on with things. He got his driving licence. By all accounts he was being an active member of society and there's been no record of him being in trouble again.'

'Something might have kicked him off.'

'You're right. Now, would you like a refill?'

'Please.' He handed her the coffee mug. Seven years ago, he wouldn't have trusted her to make him a coffee, thinking that she was about to try to end his life.

When she came back, she had added nothing more to the mug than coffee.

'Does Catherine still have her boyfriend?' she asked, skilfully bringing the conversation back round to Bracken's love life.

'She does.'

'But?'

'But what?' he said.

'There was a "but" coming there, I was sure.'

'She thinks he's going to ask her to marry him, but she's not in love with him and doesn't want to get married. In fact – and she told me this in confidence – she hasn't slept with him.'

'And you believe her?' Ailsa said, sipping her coffee.

'I've sat across from many liars in my day and I couldn't detect a lie from her. But then again, why would she take me out to the pub just to tell me she hadn't slept with him? It's none of my business, and I wouldn't have asked.'

'She was looking for your approval, Sean.'

'She doesn't need my approval.'

'She trusts you, and more to the point, she's still in love with you. That's why she wanted you to know.'

'Give over. We're friends, that's all.'

'She doesn't have female friends that she could talk to about this?'

'Of course she does.'

'There you go then.'

There was silence in the room for a moment, just the crackling of the logs burning in the fireplace disturbing the peace.

'If she's the one with feelings, or if she's feeling vulnerable because of this person, just go easy with her. You don't want to hurt her.'

'No, I don't.'

They sat and chatted for a little while about the mundane things in life.

'Do you ever feel overwhelmed working as a minister in a church, instead of being a psychologist?' he asked.

She smiled. 'I wouldn't have been much of a psychologist if I couldn't prepare myself for this life. Besides, it's a life I chose, one that I'd studied for in the hope that one day I could achieve it.'

Bracken nodded. As usual, Ailsa made sense.

'Where would Jerome Kelly be now?'

'He was staying at the Royal Edinburgh then after a while the patients would get moved out into a halfway house and then we'd work with the council to get them into sheltered housing.'

'So Kelly would be in sheltered housing right now?'

'He will be,' Ailsa said.

'For all our sakes, I hope so.'

SEVENTEEN

Bob Long came into the living room in the guest house and looked at the German shepherd lying on his side in front of the fire.

'I hope you don't mind me saying so, Ed, but I think the training's taken a downturn.'

Ed looked at his friend and shook his head. 'Let's face it, he's never going to be a movie star. But he's my boy and he'll be by my side when I hit the road.'

Bob stepped further into the room. 'What do you mean?'

'I'll be off soon.'

'Off? Where to?'

'My new mobile home will be ready this weekend. I was going to surprise Sean. And you too, of course.'

'Mission accomplished.'

'It was a last-minute thing. It got delivered

yesterday and it only takes a day to set it up. You know, connect the pipes and stuff.'

'You know I used to be a detective inspector?' Bob said.

'Aye, of course I do.'

'Well, I know shite when I see it, pal. Why don't I make us a coffee and you can spill the beans.'

'I'm that shite at lying?'

'Of course you are.' Bob stopped short before adding *'daft old bastard'* because Ed had become a friend to him.

'How about a couple of nips? I'd rather have something that will make me a bit more chilled than something that will get me buzzing. I'm already worried about what Sean's going to say.'

'Fuck me, you've not got that lassie pregnant?'

'Och, away, for God's sake. I only just met her last night. But that's just the thing.'

'Hold on. Let me get a couple of glasses from the back.'

Bob got up and left the room, and Max lifted his head to see what was going on. When he found out it was nothing, he lay back down again, took in a deep breath and let it out.

'I'm glad one of us is comfortable,' Ed said to the big dog.

Bob came back with two glasses. 'Mary asked what

these were for and I told her we were going to have a wee nip and to mind her own business.'

Ed took one of the glasses. 'What did you really say to her?'

'I told her you were in a spot of bother and it was only whisky that would take the edge off.'

Bob got the bottle and poured two measures before sitting down.

'Okay. I'm all ears.'

'I met Elizabeth online. She's younger than me, as I said, but nowadays that's not a big deal, is it?'

'Twenty years, you said.'

'Aye, but it's more like thirty years. She looks so young. Like one of those lassies you'd meet on a Russian bride site. The ones who want to come here just to get a husband.'

'She's Russian?'

'Naw, she's no' Russian. She's...' Ed stopped suddenly.

Bob leant forward a bit, as if waiting for a punch-line. 'A bloke?'

'Get a grip of yourself. I was going to say she comes from London, but something struck me. She didn't sound English. I mean, sort of posh, but not proper posh. Know what I mean?'

'Aye. Like some people from Scotland will try and

get rid of the Scottish accent so people will think they're English,' Bob said.

'Exactly. But that's not all.'

'Jesus, there's more? I thought that was it.'

'She's got a teenage son. The wee bastard's coming to live here, she says. With us. Now, don't get me wrong, I've lived with a teenage laddie – but that was my own. I've never even seen the wee snot or knew he existed, never mind been consulted on whether he could come and live with us.'

Bob swallowed the rest of the whisky. 'Christ, I need a top-up.' He got up and poured two more measures, then sat back down. 'Does she have her own place up here sorted yet?' he asked, knowing the answer.

'No. She's staying with a friend. Her brother's in hospital, as you know, but she had said he'll be looked after by another sister and their mother. She wants to come up here and live with me. She's staying with a friend until she can move into my place with her son.'

'Your place?'

'Aye. She thinks I have a big house.'

'Aw, fuck me. You didn't tell her this place is yours, did you?'

'Not quite.'

'Which means you did,' Bob said.

'Now, now, steady on. I didn't tell her I lived here. Just in Corstorphine in general.'

'Now she thinks you have a big house and she and the offspring will move in. But the fly in the ointment is, you don't have a place yet.'

'I also told her I was loaded.'

'Can this get any worse, Ed?'

'Aye, it can. And it does. I leant her some money.'

Bob chugged at the whisky. Maybe the alcohol would dull the pain when his heart gave out. 'How much?'

'A few thousand.'

'Define "a few".'

'Fifteen. Part of the money I had in the bank for my new home.'

'Christ Almighty, Ed. I was a copper for a long time and I'm going to be blunt here: you were taken to the cleaner's.'

'I know. I'll have to take out a bank loan to be able to afford my new home.'

'No, you won't. Do you think that lassie conned you?'

'Not exactly. She gave me a sob story and I fell for it. I offered her the money. She promised to pay me back when she got a job.'

'Sean's going to go mental.'

'I know he is.'

'And you know Elizabeth isn't going to pay you back.'

Ed sighed. 'I've been a stupid old man, and I think Elizabeth talks a good game.'

'Sounds like she made up a story about having a teenage son to put you off, so you'll be the one to call it off, and then you can kiss your money goodbye.'

'It worked.'

Bob smiled and drank more of his whisky. 'We can get your money back if you want.'

'Of course I want.'

'That's good. We're going to have to be careful, but you and I are going on a fishing trip. I just need some details first.'

EIGHTEEN

'Come on, I know you're in there.' The skinny man stood looking down at the figure lying prone on the settee. For all intents and purposes, the sprawled man looked like he was dead.

'Are you just going to ignore me? You can't, can you? Not me. You know I'm here and you know I'm not going anywhere. You may as well open your eyes and look at me.'

The man lying on the settee suddenly opened his eyes and stared at the bigger man. 'Well, well, look who's here. Fuck-Face himself.' He sat up so fast that Skinny thought he was going to be attacked, but the man merely got to his feet and stood looking at him.

'I'm glad to see you back, Jerome.'

Jerome Kelly smiled and patted his stomach. 'I've

been away for a while, and now I'm hungry. Show me where you keep your food.'

Skinny nodded and turned away, thinking for a moment that Kelly was about to pounce on him, but he didn't. Into the kitchen and Skinny pointed out the fridge, which was a big stainless-steel affair that didn't need any introduction.

'My-fucking-my, we have done well for ourselves, haven't we?' Kelly said. 'And by "we", I mean fucking "you".'

The skinny man felt a shiver of fear run down his spine. He had been hoping that maybe Jerome would be a changed man, that something had clicked in his head that would make him more pleasing. That the old violent man had gone for good. But now he realised that Jerome Kelly had been simmering beneath the surface.

Yet he couldn't blame anybody but himself. He'd been the one who had brought Kelly back. Had spoken to him like he could hear every word, thinking that maybe Kelly was long gone and he was wasting his time.

Then, one day, Kelly had come back. Meaner than ever. Killing was a pleasure for him, Skinny realised. And the skinny man wondered if he had let the genie out of the bottle. Then Kelly's alter ego had appeared, the soft-spoken friend. The one who had a sense of humour, the one who cared. When Skinny closed his eyes, though, he never knew which one of them was coming back.

'Help yourself,' Skinny said.

'I will. Don't you fucking worry about that. I'm hungry, so I'm going to make myself something to eat. And you'd better hope I don't burn the fucking house down while I'm cooking.'

The skinny man's face fell.

Kelly laughed. 'Don't worry, I'm only fucking with you. I know how to cook.'

'Who taught you to cook?'

Kelly looked at him as if it was a loaded question. 'Rita did. She was a good cook. You remember Rita, don't you?'

Skinny remained silent for a moment, wanting to answer but worried about upsetting Kelly.

'Yes. She was very nice. I liked her a lot.'

Kelly had opened the big fridge door. It was what the store had described as an 'American-style' fridge. Skinny had wondered what the Americans called a fridge. Just 'fridge', he thought.

Kelly brought his face round. 'You liked her a lot?' He held the fridge door open.

'I did. She was a good friend.'

'Not as much as I fucking liked her, I hope? Like

you were hoping to get your fucking end away with her or anything.'

'Nothing like that. She was your girlfriend; everybody knew that.'

'Fucking right she was.' Head back into the fridge. 'And now all those fuckers are going to be made to pay,' Kelly said, his voice echoing around beside the food.

He had obviously found something to eat, because he took out a plate and let the door close. He took the plate into the dining room and the skinny man followed. Kelly sat at the table and Skinny saw what he had taken: a roast chicken that had been half-eaten.

'Go and get us a drink,' Kelly said, starting to pull meat off the carcass. He looked at Skinny when there was no indication of movement. 'Hurry fucking up. I might choke on a bone or something.'

Skinny left the dining room, wondering if it would be feasible to take a carving knife and ram it into the other man. An idea had already formed in his head of how he would explain things to the QC at his defence. Instead, he took back nothing more dangerous than a glass of water.

'Choke on a bone,' Kelly said. 'You'd fucking like that, eh? And what's this?'

'H_2O. More commonly known as tap water. Anything else, get it yourself. I'm not your servant.'

Kelly took the glass and drank some, his beady eyes peering over the rim, staring at the skinny man.

'Not my servant? Except when you want me to kill somebody.'

Skinny laughed. 'Listen to you. You've been in hiding all this time. Hidden deep in the depths of your twin –'

'Triplet,' Kelly corrected. 'There's three of us.'

'Triplet then. Hidden away, eager to come back, but you couldn't. You had to stay in hiding, just in case they locked you up for good. And now, thanks to me, you've been given a new lease of life.'

Kelly tucked into the food as if he hadn't eaten in a very long time. It was like he was an animal.

'Are you going to sit down? Standing there fucking staring.'

Skinny sat down, not quite opposite, not wanting to be sprayed with chicken-filled spit.

'Mind and keep your appearance neat. You don't want them to know you're back.'

'Killing that old bastard is going to tip them the wink, though, don't you think?'

'Let's play it by ear.'

Skinny watched the other man eat until he felt sick. Then he got up from the table. 'What about the other woman?'

'She won't be a problem.'

'She's not a part of this.'

'I didn't say she was.'

'Then make sure you leave her be.'

Jerome Kelly kept on eating and didn't take his eyes off the skinny man until he'd left the room.

NINETEEN

Bracken felt good by the time he left Ailsa Connolly (he couldn't think of her as Anne Marshall). He had promised he would go and see her husband while he was staying over in Edinburgh, then he would go and have a meal with them both one day. Ailsa was still the most intelligent woman he had ever met.

He looked at the clock; the drive had taken a little over an hour with the blue lights flashing behind the grill on his car, since it was pretty much motorway all the way from Stirling. He'd taken the phone call while he was about ready to leave Ailsa.

'You need to come over here, Sean. You're going to want to see this.'

The road he was looking for was on the outskirts of Kirkcaldy. Strathore Road, where the Thornton Fever Hospital was, or what was left of it. The locals knew it as Strathore Asylum. It had been rundown and neglected for decades.

It was also a place where Jerome Kelly had been incarcerated for a while.

The road was long and narrow and now filled with emergency vehicles, one of which was blocking the road. Bracken spoke to the uniform and was let through.

He was met by Cameron Robb as he parked.

'What's with the fire engines?' he asked Robb.

'That's what alerted us. A passing motorist saw one of the buildings well alight. Come on in, sir. Gladstone's waiting.'

Bracken shuddered in his coat as the cold bit into him. They walked past the fire engines and the police cars. Snow had blanketed the fields around them and the rooftops, or what was left of them, behind the wall.

'How was Ailsa Connolly?' Robb asked.

'She and I had a good conversation. She gave me more of an insight into this Kelly bloke.'

'That he's a raving nut-job?'

'More that he's a lot more cunning than he made himself out to be, I think.'

Gladstone was standing looking at the smouldering ruins of what was once a house in the grounds of the hospital. He had a face like a Crowded House album cover.

'There's an eclectic collection of buildings in there. It was like a smaller version of Gogarburn,' he said to Bracken as the big detective approached.

'And somebody was burnt in there,' Bracken replied, nodding to where firefighters were busy with their equipment.

'Not in there, no. In the house. This bonfire here was a beacon to summon us.' Gladstone looked at Bracken. 'To make sure we came and found what he had left for us.'

'Another victim, I presume.'

'Fuck, aye. He's ramping it up now, Sean.'

'If you mean Jerome Kelly, then he's nowhere to be found.'

'That's because he was here sticking it to somebody.'

'Who is it? Do we know?'

They were walking along the road now, trying not to fall on their arses.

'Aye. Claire Thompson's mother. The woman we were trying to get hold of to tell her that her daughter was murdered. Now she's a victim herself.' Gladstone slipped and blindly reached out and grabbed hold of Bracken's arm. 'Bastard place.'

'Were there footprints or tracks of any kind?' Bracken asked.

'Nothing we could find, but the fire brigade have

been all over here. Nothing significant near the crime scene either. Come and take a look.'

There were two buildings, one of them large and the other much smaller. Two separate dwellings. The bigger house had been set alight as well, but the fire had been brought under control.

'After the call was made, the firefighters were here within minutes. The hospital was well alight, but the house had just been started. The superintendent lived in the big house, back in the day. Head maintenance guy, in the smaller house.'

A uniform was standing guard outside what appeared to be an old stone cottage, painted white.

'In here,' Gladstone said unnecessarily as they fought their way past the busy firefighters and the hoses.

Inside the small house, a figure sat tied to a chair, her head slumped forward. Tape had been used to secure a plastic bag round her head, just like with the other victims.

'Audrey Thompson. Her driving licence is in her pocket. I had her name run through the system and it spat out a wee nugget of information.'

Bracken's breath blew out into the cold air. 'I thought she lived in Glenrothes?'

'She does, according to her licence. But come and take a look at this.' Gladstone led Bracken through to another room. An old man lay on a bed, his head also wrapped in a plastic bag.

'Guess who it is, Sean,' Gladstone said.

'He's Peter Solomon, Rita Solomon's father. Rita was the victim from thirty years ago,' Robb said.

Gladstone tutted. 'Fuck me. Is your name Sean? Indeed it is not. When I say, "Guess, Sean," I am not in fact saying, "You fucking fire in with the answer whenever you feel like it, Cameron." Bad wee bastard.'

Gladstone looked at Bracken. 'That ruined the surprise, did it not?'

'As long as we get there in the end, sir.'

'I don't know about you, but I think that's like when you ask somebody, "Oh, did you know so-and-so died?", maybe a famous actor or something, and the smartarse replies, "Yes, I did." I fucking hate that.' Back to Robb. 'You've just had any brownie points you'd built up shot down in flames. Jumping in like that with the fucking answer. Wee baw-bag.'

'And Audrey Thompson is connected how?' Bracken asked.

'She's Peter Solomon's other daughter. Rita's older sister. It looks like they were staying here, maybe to look after the old man. There was a "For Sale" sign standing out front until it was knocked down by an errant hose. I called the estate agent and he said the old man lived here with his daughter.'

'And Claire's his granddaughter,' Robb added.

'Can you no' fucking help yourself?' Gladstone said to him.

'DCI Bracken would have worked that one out anyway, sir,' Robb said in his own defence.

'Aye, but you can't help it, eh? Fucking jumping in like that. You're like the wee laddie in class shouting out instead of putting his hand up. Try and keep yourself under control.' Gladstone shook his head.

'I wonder why Kelly's killing Rita's family?' Bracken said. 'Ailsa said that Rita was his best friend.'

'We could ask him if we found the bastard,' said Gladstone. 'I for one think he killed those women. He pretends he's daft and then everybody believes him, but in fact he's a fucking psycho.'

'Could be. He has a split personality disorder. Maybe it lay dormant for years and now it's come to the surface for whatever reason.'

They heard shouts from outside.

'See?' Gladstone said to Robb. 'Even the fire service think you're no' all there. Shouting out like that. Coffees are on you for the rest of the month.'

A firefighter appeared at the door. 'You'd better see this, sir,' she said to Gladstone.

The detectives followed her outside and they trudged through the snow and mud again.

'If he falls on his arse, I'm going to piss myself laughing,' Robb said to Bracken as they took the lead.

'I heard that, ya wee bastard.'

The firefighter led them to the house that had been on fire. 'In here,' she said.

The room was still smouldering and looked like somebody had painted it black. Front and centre was the charred form of something that had once been human.

'Petrol can over there. A really old one, like from back in the day when they were made of metal,' she explained.

'Could he have poured it over himself?' Gladstone asked. 'Or herself, whatever the case may be.'

'It's possible, of course. Or somebody could have poured it over him. Or her. The body's so badly burnt that you'll need the pathologist to make out the sex.'

'Do you think that could be Jerome Kelly?' Gladstone said.

'It's hard to say,' Bracken said, 'when it's curled into a foetal shape like that.'

'He's probably had a lot of his body burnt off, though.' Gladstone looked at the face, the teeth gleaming through the blackened skull.

'His skeletal remains will be able to tell us when he's been put on the mortuary table.'

Gladstone thanked the fire officer and then the

detectives left the smoky building. Outside, snow was coming down now.

'Let's just say that's Kelly in there,' said Gladstone. 'What was he trying to tell us? He's killed his friend's sister and father and now he just wants to end it all? Why didn't he jump in front of a train?'

Then a thought struck Bracken. 'How did he get here?'

'Does anybody know if Kelly has a driving licence or not?'

'He does,' Bracken said. 'We already checked.'

'The car sitting there belongs to Audrey Thompson. There's no record of the old man having a car now,' Robb said.

'Then whose car is that?' Bracken said, pointing to a small blue saloon car.

'Christ,' Gladstone said, looking at Robb.

'I assumed it belonged to the owner of the house. Let me run the plates.' Robb called it in and the two older detectives stood around in the falling snow waiting for the answer.

'The car belongs to a man called Stewie Anderson.'

TWENTY

Bracken told Gladstone he would liaise with him later. They would contact a next of kin for Anderson and prepare them for what may or may not be bad news. Asking for dental records was always an ice breaker, and the waiting game afterwards. Toss a coin: heads it's your son, tails it could be a complete stranger. The odds were always in favour of the house.

Back in the incident room, Bracken took his coat off and flopped into one of the office chairs at a desk. Izzie Khan was at the whiteboard with DC Lennox Docherty. Jimmy Sullivan was on the phone and Tam Gale was getting wired into a Greggs pie.

'Doctor said I have to eat several small meals a day,' he explained to Bracken. 'My blood sugar gets low.'

'Pity your belly didn't get low, though.'

'I'm a shadow of my former self,' Gale said.

Jimmy scoffed as he set the phone down. 'Shadow? Come on, Tam. The *Titanic* didn't make as much of a shadow.'

'That's not very nice,' Gale replied, wiping grease off his chin. He took a swig from the Coke bottle sitting on his desk and was about to belch when he saw Bracken watching him. He ducked his head under the table and Bracken thought for a moment that the man was puking, but then they all heard the muted growl as a rapid explosion of air escaped from him.

'God Almighty,' Bracken said. 'I'm surprised you didn't shite yourself as well.'

'It's all about body control,' Gale replied.

'You're giving everybody the boak, Tam,' Sullivan said, fanning a hand across in front of his face. 'Stinking the bloody place out.'

Bracken updated the team on what they had found at the old Strathmore hospital.

'I was just on the phone with the sheltered housing place at the Grange, and the warden said Kelly hasn't lived there for a long time,' Doc said.

Bracken looked puzzled. 'What do you mean? That's part of him being in the community, isn't it?'

'He was released into the care of his sister.'

'He didn't have a sister.'

'Somebody came and took him, sir. A female. She said she would keep in touch with the warden, but she never did. And things being the way they are, well, out of sight, out of mind.'

'What was this sister's name?' Bracken asked.

'Elizabeth. No last name.'

'Claire lived at home with her mother,' Izzie said. 'I was looking her up on social media. She was an influencer.'

'Oh, God, one of those people who think every-body should fawn over them, and the dafties who hang on to their every word,' Gale said.

'You're just jealous, Tam,' Izzie said. 'Claire prob-ably earned a fortune.'

Gale picked up at that. 'Maybe I could become an influencer.'

'You're already an influencer,' Bracken said. 'You influence people in handcuffs to get in the back of the car.'

'I was looking at Claire's website,' Izzie said, 'and she has podcasts. I listened to one in particular. It's titled, *My Aunt's Killer*. She doesn't go into too many specifics, but she talks about how she thinks she knows who killed her aunt thirty years ago.'

'She must have been going to make money from the story of how Kelly killed Rita Solomon in Craigtoun. Maybe Kelly found out and decided to get rid of Claire and her mother,' Bracken said. 'Not to mention Old Man Solomon. We need to find Kelly. He's on the warpath and he might not have the wherewithal to be able to stop.'

He asked Izzie, 'Did this podcast mention anything specific? Like, did she mention Kelly by name?'

'No. She was just giving snippets, like a preview. She said that she was preparing it and that it was coming soon. And a book too.'

Bracken perked up at that. 'A book? So she would have notes and maybe a manuscript that's partially written, something like that?'

'Possibly.'

'Stewie Anderson worked for the production company that's filming the DIY show,' Gale said. 'Did you see the way he was acting at the scene when he and the others found Claire? Hardly a bumbling wreck.'

'He might not have been if he already knew she was in there,' Doc said.

'But then again, all they saw was a woman sitting in a chair with a bag over her head. Hard to identify her,' Bracken said.

'His car is registered in Fife,' Sullivan said.

'I know. Let me go and make the phone call to Fife,' Bracken said, getting up and stretching. 'I'll see how they got on at his address.'

TWENTY-ONE

Gladstone didn't have a problem with control, more a problem with smoking.

'Filthy habit, the wife says,' he said, cranking down the window. 'Then she asks me when I'm going to start taking care of myself. If you quit smoking, you start eating like a bastard. Hobson's choice: lungs turn black and fall out, or belly expands like a balloon and explodes. Like Mr Creosote. Ever seen that Monty Python film, *The Meaning of Life*?'

Cameron Robb was navigating the car round Glenrothes.

'You're no' in a fucking huff, I hope?'

'What? Oh, no, sir. Sorry. I was miles away. And yes, I did see that film. Years ago. Nearly pissed myself.'

'There's no talent like those blokes nowadays.

They knew how to make you laugh back then. It's all filth now.'

The snow had taken a tea break and now the roads were slushy and the tyres made a sound like they were buzzing with electricity as Robb drove along.

'Christ, you're usually yappy when we're out and about. You wearing Y-fronts that are two sizes too small or something?'

'Just thinking, sir.'

'Women or football?'

'Not women, plural. Woman, singular,' Robb said, booting it across a roundabout in front of a tipper lorry.

'You wondering what kind of wreath she'll send to your funeral after you get us fucking killed?'

'Plenty of room there.'

'His fucking eyes lit up there. Bastard put the boot down when he saw you approaching. Do me a favour and choose another day to try and prove you're invincible.'

Gladstone went as far as taking a cigarette out of the crushed box he kept in his pocket. His 'lucky' box of ciggies, the ones that would have been behind glass with the words 'in case of emergency break glass' written on it if they had been a fire hose. Gladstone felt that almost having his arse felt by a twenty-ton piece of flying metal on wheels with some mental skinhead bastard behind the wheel constituted an emergency.

'If Chief Superintendent Dixon upstairs gets a report that I was smoking in a car, tell him you saw fuck all, or plead insanity. Or tell him you valiantly tried to wrestle the pack from my hands, but I told you I carry a sidearm and made threatening gestures with one hand in my pocket.'

'He'll think you were playing pocket tennis again.'

'What do you mean *again*, ya cheeky bastard?' Gladstone lit up and puffed on the cigarette and tried blowing smoke out the window but missed. He waved his hand in front of him, trying to dispel the evidence.

'I'm sure old Dafty Dixon won't care that you were honking out a pool car, sir. He's got one foot out the door. Retirement's knocking and he's already about to pull the trigger on buying a holiday home in Spain.'

'Aye, well, good luck with that, I say. It's not as easy as it once was, now that we're not kissing it up the Germans, or whoever else is in charge of what's collectively known as Club EU.'

'Still. Let the old boy have his dream, eh? I mean, Pettycur Bay caravan park doesn't have the same appeal, I'm sure.'

'Nothing wrong with a caravan holiday, son. Me and the wife take our grand bairns up to Pitlochry in the summer.'

'Not the same as seeing scantily clad women on a Spanish beach.'

'That's enough of that talk. Besides, I'm past all that. I'm sure Dixon is too.' Gladstone shook his head. 'Clearly you're no'. I can picture you now, skulking about a beach wearing socks with your sandals and taking photos of the "seagulls".' He used one hand for air quotes, his other fingers clinging on to his cigarette like it was the last life jacket on a sinking ship.

'That's disgusting, sir, if you don't mind me saying. Wearing sandals with socks.'

'Mark my words, boy, that's a slippery slope, going to Club Perv on your own.'

'I wouldn't be going on my own.'

'And now we come to it, that young lassie who's been taking all of your attention. What's her name again?'

'There's quite a few; I can't remember all of their names,' Robb said.

'You don't even have the decency to pull a fucking beamer when you talk like that. You know fine well who I'm talking about. The forensics lassie. Quite a few lassies indeed. You know there's a cream for that.'

'Her name's Lynn Shaw. And we've been seeing each other for a couple of months.'

'Aye, that's her name. Lynn. Poor lassie. It's a good thing Police Scotland's an equal opportunity employer, so she can bring her guide dug to work. Imagine her being able to see your ugly coupon.'

'That's not very nice, sir. But if you start having a mid-life crisis, she's got a sister.'

'If I do have a mid-life crisis, I'll stick with buying a Porsche 911, thank you very much. Imagine my wife catching me with a younger woman? I'd never walk straight again and I'd be able to get the lead singer part in a Bee Gees tribute band.'

They were looking for an address in Leslie, just north of Glenrothes. Robb drove under the aqueduct and up the hill. Left into the High Street.

'Humped crossing, the sign says,' Gladstone said. 'I thought it said "numpty crossing". I wonder how many numpties live here?'

'They might be thinking, here's a couple of numpties from the polis coming.'

'Speak for yourself.'

The house they were looking for was in a street on the right. It was semi-detached and looked clean from the outside, with a newish car parked in the small driveway.

They got out and walked up a pathway that had been shovelled with little enthusiasm. Robb knocked on the door with a force halfway between a Jehovah's Witness and *Let me in or I'll huff and I'll puff and I'll blow your house down.*

A woman answered, her thick eyebrows knitted together as if she had just glued them on and her mouth screwed up in a scowl that would melt wallpaper.

'Oh. Fucking polis,' she said, before Gladstone lifted his warrant card.

'Are you Mrs Anderson?' Robb said, jumping in before Gladstone had a chance to unleash some sarky reply.

'Aye. And?'

'And we'd like to come in and talk to you about your son. Or we can stand here on the doorstep, where my voice will no doubt have to be raised against the wind and your neighbours will be getting a free show.'

The woman tutted. 'What's the little bastard gone and done now? Always fucking about with a rum crowd, that one.'

She stood back and Gladstone got a view of what Stewie must have had to endure growing up. Inside, there was probably a belt waiting to teach the miscreant a lesson.

He and Robb walked in. The smell of something heating in the oven wafted through, and suddenly Gladstone felt his stomach growl. Whatever was being heated up, he wouldn't mind a piece of it at that moment.

'To the right,' the woman instructed, as if the detectives were about to go raking through her knickers drawer.

They turned into a small living room, big enough for a settee, a chair and a TV, with a couple of accent tables. Maybe it had been a bedroom at one point and had been turned into a TV room. Maybe it was Stewie's and had been converted before the door had had a chance to bang his arse on the way out.

Mrs Anderson lay claim to the big leather chair and looked at the two men as if a game of musical chairs was about to begin. She sat forward, like this would give her a leg up when the music started up again, but it was only the sound of the boiler kicking in that disturbed their peace. The detectives sat down on the settee.

'Come on then, out with it. What's he done?'

'Do you live alone?' Gladstone said.

Mrs Anderson looked at him like this was a bad chat-up line gone wrong and she was about to let him have it.

'Why? Somebody trying to drop me in it with the council? I pay my fair share. Everything's above board here. Stewie doesn't live here anymore.'

'It's nothing to do with that. I just wanted to know if there's anybody else living here.'

'No. Just me. His father fucked off a long time ago, the hoor.'

'I'm sorry to have to tell you this,' said Gladstone,

'but a body has been found badly burned. We have reason to believe it's Stewie.'

Mrs Anderson sat still for a moment, looking at the blank TV screen as if somebody was going to pop on and tell her this was a joke. But nobody did, and the two detectives sat there waiting for a response.

'Why would you think it's him?' she said, all the wind gone out of her sails.

'His car was at the scene. There was a fire and more fatalities. Unfortunately, we have to ask family members for dental records. That means us contacting his dentist.'

'Aye, I know what that means. I watch *CSI*. I have the contact details here. We have the same dentist, just round the corner, even though he doesn't live here anymore.'

'Where did he live?' Robb asked. 'His car is registered here.'

She looked at him for a moment as if he had actually had the audacity to come right out and accuse her of being a council tax cheat.

'Not here. With that lassie he was so enamoured with.' Her voice had lost some of its edge now, and Gladstone thought that this must be a rare occasion. Mrs Anderson didn't look like a woman who would be able to keep quiet for long.

'Who would that be?' Gladstone said. 'Claire Thompson?'

'Aye. He said they were working on something.' She looked down at the carpet for a moment before making eye contact with Gladstone. 'How did he get burnt? What was he doing?'

'We're not sure of the exact details just yet, but he was found in a house that had caught fire.'

'Was this Mason lassie hurt as well?'

'Not that we're aware of just now. We just have Stewie's car; that's why we're here,' Robb said. 'This Mason lassie would be Stella Mason, I assume? The woman he worked with?'

'Aye, that's her. Right flighty wee besom. I didn't like her at all. There was something about her. Something feral. Very guarded she was. But when your uncle is a well-known TV presenter, you could go to work with a face like Krakatoa and nobody would say boo.'

'Her uncle is...?' Gladstone asked.

'Desmond Rough, of course,' she answered, like the older detective should have known this. 'He's the only one who made good in that family. Two of the daughters disappear one day, never to be heard from again. Runaways, they said. It all faded from the news. Nobody cared. As far as I know, they've never been heard from since. That was over thirty years ago.'

'You wouldn't happen to know where this Stella Mason lives, do you?'

'No. I met her once. She worked beside him, but she hadn't been there that long.' She paused for a moment. 'Oh, wait. He did mention it. He said that the production company was just starting out so they were cutting back on spending, just until they got on their feet. They were renting a flat down in Leith to save money on hotel bills. I think I have it written down.'

She got to her feet and left the living room, then came back a few minutes later with an address book. She flipped through the pages until she came to the name she was looking for. 'There it is, Stella Mason. Sandport, in Leith.'

Robb scribbled it down in his notebook.

'Was the old boy hurt?' Mrs Anderson asked.

'Excuse me?' Gladstone said.

'Old Mr Solomon. I met him a few times. Stewie had problems with his car at times, and I used to drive him along to the Solomons' house. That's where Claire lived, with her mother. They looked after the old man. But the stories he came out with. It would make the hair stand up on a billiard ball.'

'What do you mean?' Gladstone asked, scooting himself further to the edge of the cushion.

'His other daughter was murdered by that freak Jerome Kelly. He was put away in the nut house.

Craigtoun. Ironic, isn't it? He killed Rita there when it was an empty mansion, and he was locked up in the old asylum next to where Solomon lives now. Then Kelly was sent back to Craigtoun when it had been converted.

'You know, old Peter Solomon was the superinten-dent at the Strathore Asylum. Solomon himself agreed that Kelly shouldn't have been placed where he was the superintendent, but back then I don't think anybody gave a shit. Solomon told me that Kelly would beg to speak to him when he was in there. Solomon was raging of course, and it took a while for him to speak to Kelly, but then one night he relented and sat down with Kelly. Solomon told me he looked Kelly in the eyes and asked him why he had killed his daughter. Kelly looked right back and said he didn't kill her, that Rita was his friend. Then Solomon asked him one question: who did then?'

Gladstone realised he had been holding his breath, and he let it go as he asked the next question. 'What was the answer?'

'Kelly told him. But Solomon scoffed. He accused Kelly of lying to cover his own arse. Years later, though, when Kelly was out in the care of the community, Solomon bumped into him and he couldn't believe the transformation. Kelly had smartened himself up. You wouldn't think it was the same man. And Solomon asked him again, and – bearing in mind, this was many years later – Kelly gave him the same answer: Audrey did. Audrey killed her own sister, Rita. With the help of her boyfriend.'

'Did he say who this boyfriend was?' Robb asked. If anybody in the room had a pin, there would be no doubt they would all hear it should it be dropped.

Mrs Anderson shook her head. 'No. But Kelly said he was there with them at the time. Kelly didn't know they had killed Rita. They scarpered and left him, and when the police turned up, the others were gone. And Kelly was arrested.'

TWENTY-TWO

Bracken sat with Jimmy Sullivan in the car outside the offices of Sunrise Productions. They weren't much to write home about, and Sullivan stated that he had seen better brothels.

'On TV, of course,' he elaborated.

'I should bloody well hope so,' Bracken said, but he had to agree. The property, on Bath Road in Leith, could have done with being refurbished with an excavator and a few sticks of dynamite.

There was a tenement standing alone on the corner of Bath Road and Constitution Street, like a poor man's version of the Flatiron Building in New York. There was a closed pub on the corner, the 'For Sale' sign looking like it had seen better days. The back of the building that faced the Forth looked like something had ripped the arse off it a long time ago, and the ivy that had climbed all over it was like a fetid bandage on a torn-off limb.

There was a yard right behind the tenement building, hiding behind an iron fence that looked like it was there to keep people in rather than out. Within the perimeter, a long Portakabin was over to the left – the offices, Bracken assumed – while a large warehouse sat further back. In front of the offices a couple of expensive-looking cars were mixed in with the bread-and-butter vehicles.

Sullivan had parked beside a Mercedes SUV.

'Nice motor,' he said as they got out.

'I'm sure there are a few of those going in the druggie auction they're having next month in Glasgow. You could be driving about in a pimped-up Merc with blacked-out windows.'

'I don't think it's really my style.'

'You'd get more respect when you drop the kids off at school.'

'That's true. Best parking space. Nice one.'

Bracken looked around, past the fence, across the road to the new flats there. 'That used to be a builders' merchant,' he said. 'I nicked somebody in there. Stupid bastard decided to run inside and got cornered. There's big changes going on down here.' He turned back to the Portakabin. 'Let's get in here and have a chat.'

Snow lay on the ground, dissected only by tyre

tracks. Bracken climbed the steps to the door marked 'Reception' and opened it. Inside, the warmth greeted them like a favourite aunt.

'Can I help you?' asked a woman sitting behind a desk. There was a computer on her desk and she looked like a pit bull that had been taken away from its favourite toy.

'We'd like to speak with Desmond Rough,' Bracken said as they showed her their warrant cards.

'I'll call,' she said, picking up a phone handset.

'No need,' Desmond Rough said, walking through a doorway from a narrow corridor. 'Come this way, gentlemen.'

He showed them along to a small lounge area, where it was clear people had been smoking. And eating. Overflowing ashtrays, empty beer cans, discarded coffee cups and food wrappers were scattered around.

'Care for a coffee?' Rough asked. Bracken looked at the manky mugs hiding amongst the plastic ones and decided he wasn't going to chance it.

'I can send Mary out to the little lunch van outside,' Rough said, like a door-to-door salesman who had just been told to shove the vacuum cleaner nozzle up his arse and was trying for one last pitch.

'We're good,' Bracken said, thinking he wasn't ready for a cup of botulism.

'Then please sit.'

Bracken looked at Sullivan, who looked like he had just been asked to sleep on the wet patch.

'We'll stand,' he said.

'Fair enough, but I'll take the weight off my feet, if you don't mind.'

'Knock yourself out.'

Rough sat down heavily on the one office chair in the tight room and it made an imploding sound and rolled back a couple of feet before Rough stopped it.

'This is about young Claire,' he said. 'Tragic. Just a tragedy.'

'Doesn't necessarily crap all over your ratings, does it?' Sullivan said. 'I mean, viewers will be throwing parties when that episode comes on. "Look, that's where they found the body!" they'll be saying.'

'It's unfortunate, but that's the way of the world nowadays, Inspector. People love a disaster.'

'It's all blood money,' Sullivan said. 'Media bastards.'

'It allows us to make shows,' Rough said, the smile sticking to his face as if it was being held there by Blu Tack.

'Give me good old Auntie Beeb any day. You pay your licence and you get your shows without those bloody adverts. Tell me, why *do* we have to watch adverts when we pay a license? We're paying the bill,

so why do we have to watch the drivel they show?'
Sullivan was warming to his subject and Bracken
wondered if the other detective thought Desmond
Rough was solely responsible for his having to sit
through overpaid actors endorsing adult pads and the
like.

'But we digress,' Bracken said, stepping in before
Sullivan could draw his baton and kneecap Rough
with it. 'How well did you know Claire Thompson?'

'I answered the questions the other detective had
for me. The fa...er, big one. What's his name again?'

'Detective Sergeant Gale?' Bracken said.

Rough snapped his fingers. 'Yes! Him. Nice
enough bloke, don't get me wrong, but a walking heart
attack. He needs to shed a few. Not being snotty, but I
was heading down that road myself and would have
been twice my size if I hadn't reined it in. He needs to
cut out the pies. Maybe take up walking or something.
But yes, I answered his questions.'

'Humour us. How well did you know Claire?'

'I didn't know her at all. Poor girl.'

'What about her mother?' Bracken looked at the
older man. He seemed physically fit for his age, which
was around fifty, if Wikipedia was to be believed, or
mid-fifties, if the online source was talking pish. Either
way, Bracken could see that big money could help stave
off being measured for a coffin.

'Audrey Thompson? I didn't know her either.'

'You ever heard the name Peter Solomon?' Sullivan asked.

Rough looked up at the ceiling as if he was thinking about what he should have for dinner. A plate of carrots and broccoli, if his drivel about eating healthily was to be believed. Then he looked Sullivan in the eyes.

'I don't recall anybody with that name. Who is he?'

'Not important. What's Stewie Anderson like to work with?'

'Stewie? He's fine. He can be a bit moody, but sometimes we have a laugh. I hope he's not in trouble?'

'Let's just say we're waiting on somebody to come back with some details about him. Stella Mason, your other production assistant?'

'Stella's pleasant and hard working. We've taken them on as property managers, and so far they've done a sterling job.'

'Is she here?'

'No, she's out and about. She and Stewie travel all over. After we finish filming at the cottage where Claire was found, we'll be doing another one, but first of all we have to match up the next couple with their new holiday home. So Stella is out and about with Stewie. They don't report to me, but I'm sure we can find out where they are at this moment, if they're somewhere with mobile service.'

'Who do they report to then?' Bracken asked. 'The other member of your staff? The snooty one, as one of my officers described him.' Gale's actual description had been *'toffee-nosed bastard'*.

'Yes. Bernie liaises with them. That's why he was with them when Claire was found.'

'And you just happened to tag along?'

'They do the ground work, and I come along nearer the time of filming, so I get a feel for the place.'

'Have you any idea of where they were meant to be going today?' Sullivan asked, comparing this man to something that a dog had left behind and was now stuck in the tread of his shoes.

'None. Stella and Stewie are pretty much freelancers. They do all the searching for the properties.'

'And they were the ones who found that little house outside Edinburgh?' Sullivan said.

'Yes, of course.'

'How well do you know Bernie Appleton?'

'I've known him for years. It was only last year that we decided to get this production company off the ground. He helped secure finances.'

'Where is he now?'

'Out and about. The very nature of this work means we're not tied to a desk all day.'

'Did he know Claire?'

'I'm sure your detective asked him the same question when he interviewed Bernie at the Royal.'

'That's just the thing: when my officers got there, he'd already been discharged. Now we're trying to find an address for him so we can interview him.'

'I can give you his address.' Rough grabbed a piece of paper from his desk and wrote it down and passed it over to Bracken.

'What about a phone number?' Sullivan asked.

'He's lost his phone. They were out scouting locations and he lost it. I'll have to get him a disposable phone because he's already lost two phones this year. I swear if his head wasn't screwed on...' Rough shook his head, as if showing the policemen that his own head was indeed screwed on properly.

'Thanks. We might have to ask you some more questions. Please be available,' Bracken said.

'Always. Please pop in anytime.'

Outside, back in the car, Bracken's phone rang. 'Hello?'

'*Sean. Your favourite superintendent here,*' DSup Gladstone said.

'How are things over in Fife?'

'*As that jumped-up fanny Desmond Rough might say, spiffing. Young Cameron and I have had an interesting morning. Turns out, Stewie Anderson was living with Claire Thompson and her mother, Audrey. They were all looking out for old Peter Solomon. Solomon was the superintendent when Strathore was open. He stayed in the house when the hospital closed and bought it from the council. But he was elderly and his mind was slipping a few gears. He told Stewie Anderson's mother about the murder. Mrs Anderson would drive Stewie there sometimes and she and the old boy would sit and have a chin wag.'*

'This is all hearsay, sir. Who is this boyfriend?'

'I know that. And she didn't know who the boyfriend was. Neither did Old Man Solomon. Either that or he kept it to himself.'

'I'd like to track down Jerome Kelly now, but nobody knows where he is.'

'Keep at it, Sean. Keep in touch.'

'Will do, sir.'

Gladstone hung up and Bracken looked at the piece of paper that Rough had given him. On it was the same address he'd been to the day before. Leon Harris's.

TWENTY-THREE

Back to Sandport, two minutes' drive from Bath Road along Salamander Street.

Sullivan pulled in through the gates to the private estate and parked in a parking space next to a red Jeep Renegade. The lights flashed on the Jeep as they got out, careful not to slip on the icy road. Bracken did a double-take when he saw the man walking across to the small SUV.

'Leon!' he said.

Leon Harris looked blankly at him for a moment, then recognition kicked in.

'Sean! What are you doing here?'

'I was coming down to talk to somebody. In fact, he should be known to you.'

'Oh, yeah? How come?'

'Because you live in the same flat. Along with Stella Mason.'

'What's his name?'

'Bernie Appleton.'

Leon stared at him for a moment. 'Never heard of him.'

'Are you sure? I got his address from a close friend of his.'

Leon laughed. 'I think I would know if another man was living in the flat.'

'What about Stella? She just a friend of yours, Leon?'

The smaller man had a bemused look on his face. 'I don't know anybody called Stella Mason. I have a flat-mate called Elizabeth.'

Sullivan watched as Bracken walked closer to the little man. 'Why did you tell me you were the manager of the Festival Theatre when you clearly aren't?'

Leon let his shoulders slump a little. 'I didn't get the job. Simple as that. I felt embarrassed. However, I am planning on buying a little theatre, where I can be my own boss. I was going to tell Catherine, but I had to find the right moment. I'm sure you understand.'

'Is Stella in right now?'

'Her name is Elizabeth, I just said. The flat is empty. Now, if you'll excuse me, Sean, I have a meeting with a bank manager.'

Bracken stood back as Leon got into the car, and he drove away, honking the horn and waving.

'Little bastard,' Bracken said.

'What the hell was all that about?' Sullivan said.

Bracken looked at the piece of paper in his hand. 'Desmond Rough gave me this address. I was here before looking for Leon. Bernie Appleton lives here too.' Bracken nodded to the back end of the red car as it left the street. 'There goes Bernie Appleton, aka Leon Harris.'

'He's the bloke we're looking for?'

'I think so. Come on, let's go and see if Stella Mason really is out and about. Or somebody called Elizabeth.'

They walked through the snow to the stairway door and Bracken pressed a few buzzers until somebody answered and let them in.

They went up to the door of the flat they were looking for. It hadn't been closed properly and the smell hit Bracken right away. He took nitrile gloves out of his pocket and nodded for Sullivan to do the same.

The smell was worse inside. Both men drew their batons. The bathroom on the right was empty; same with the bedroom on the left. The next bedroom too. That left the living room, straight ahead.

Stella Mason was sitting on a dining chair in the

middle of the room, a plastic bag tied firmly round her throat with tape. More tape had been wrapped round her chest, keeping her upright. Bracken rushed forward and dug his fingers into the plastic, but he couldn't get them through.

'Get me a knife!' Bracken ordered.

Sullivan reached into his pocket and brought out a work knife, flicking the blade out.

Bracken took it and cut the plastic, but it was obvious Stella was dead, the stench of her death filling the flat.

'You didn't tell me you carried a knife like this,' Bracken said.

'You never asked.'

Bracken made a face. 'Call it in.'

He took his own phone out and called control and gave them the registration number of the little red Jeep. It didn't take long to get the answer.

'It belongs to Stella here,' he said to Sullivan when the other man disconnected the call.

'Elizabeth was just a made-up name for Stella. Why, though?'

'I can tell you why,' another voice said.

Then they both realised there was a presence behind them. Sullivan lifted his baton while Bracken held up the knife.

'Whoa, whoa, what the hell?'

The man stood looking at them and held up his hands.

'What are you doing here, Dad?' Bracken asked.

TWENTY-FOUR

'I nearly shat myself,' Ed Bracken said. 'I came round to see Elizabeth, just to have a wee chat with her. I didn't do that!' He pointed to the corpse sitting in the chair. Bracken stood in front of the dead woman, blocking his father's view.

'Who's Elizabeth?' Sullivan asked.

'She's Elizabeth!' Ed said. His face was ashen now.

'You know her?' Bracken asked.

'Yes. She's the woman I've been seeing. Online, up until yesterday. I came round here to tell her I couldn't do it anymore. She told me her teenage son is coming up from London and I can't deal with that. I also wanted to ask for my money back.'

'What money?'

'She was toiling. Her brother is ill, and she's on the verge of getting kicked out of her place, so she wanted to come up here to start a new life. I gave her money, just until she got on her feet. She promised to give it back to me when she got a job.'

'How much?'

'Fifteen big ones. It was from the insurance payout for my house. The money I was saving for my new one. I can't afford my new house now.'

'Aw, fucking hell, Dad. She conned you.'

'I can see that now.'

'Fifteen grand. You were obviously thinking with your small brain.'

'Sir, don't give him a hard time,' Sullivan said. 'These women are experts at what they do. We know from experience.'

'Aye, I suppose. Daft old sod.'

'I didn't kill her,' Ed said again. 'We were talking and then she got a call. Said somebody was coming and to hide in the bedroom. I went into the built-in wardrobe. I thought, *Christ, she's married. Her husband's coming.* So I got in there and tried to keep my breathing quiet. Then there was arguing and the sounds of a struggle. Then nothing. I heard somebody moving about and then he was talking. On the phone, it sounded like. He said something like, "You'd better get over here. I've done something."

'A few minutes later, the front door opened and somebody else came in. He almost shrieked, his voice was that high-pitched at first, until the other one told him to shut the fuck up, they would deal with it. Then it went quiet and the door closed. I waited again and then I heard movement and the door closed again. I stayed in there. I'll admit I was shit scared. I couldn't move. Then when you came in, I thought they were back, until I heard you talking. Just as well I didn't bring Max. He would have given the game away.'

'Or chewed their balls off.'

'If they'd touched him, I'd have *booted* their balls off. As it was, being here on my own, I couldn't fight off a killer.'

'You did the right thing, Dad. I'm glad you're safe. I think Stella Mason was out to con people out of money. And Leon Harris knows why.'

'Leon? What's he got to do with this?'

'He was here.'

'Jesus. You think he killed Elizabeth? Or Stella? Whoever?'

'Possibly.'

Just then, the front door opened and two uniformed officers came in, batons drawn.

'You don't need those,' Bracken said. 'DI Sullivan here called it in.'

'No, sir, we got a treble-nine call saying somebody had been murdered here.'

'Just like the last time,' Bracken answered, almost under his breath.

'I'm sorry?'

'Nothing.' Bracken looked at Sullivan. 'Just like thirty years ago. History repeating itself. A call is made to the police, and they turn up and find Jerome Kelly standing over Rita Solomon.'

'What's the connection?' Sullivan asked.

'I think Leon Harris is Jerome Kelly.'

Bracken walked out of the room, taking his phone out. He made a call and it went to voicemail.

'Catherine? When you get this, call me. It's urgent.'

TWENTY-FIVE

Catherine Bracken looked at the phone in her hand and was about to answer it when something told her not to. This was her night out with Leon and she didn't want to have to lie to her ex-husband. If she mentioned the date, then he might say something to her that would derail her plans for tonight. She had spent all day in her office thinking about this. Leon wasn't going to be happy, but it wasn't her job in life to make him happy.

She did answer the phone when it buzzed and she saw Leon's name come up. The text simply said, *Downstairs.*

Coming, she replied. She picked up her keys, slipped her coat on and left the apartment. She couldn't see him at first because of the blacked-out windows, then the window buzzed down on the Range

Rover's passenger side and the little man smiled out at her.

'Nice car,' she said, climbing in.

'It's a friend's,' he explained, guiding the big car out of the back car park of her building.

They made idle chitchat and Catherine smiled as the Range Rover glided up Leith Walk, ticking along without missing a heartbeat.

'This is a nice car, Leon,' she said again. Her stomach was churning now and it wasn't from excitement. It was apprehension, the thought of how she was going to let him down gently if he broached the subject of their exchanging vows.

'It belongs to a friend of mine. He said I can borrow it anytime.' He smiled and reached a hand over to hers. It was hot and clammy, like he'd just had it down the front of his trousers. That very thought made her take her hand away, not quite snapping it back.

She turned and looked out the window and felt Leon's right foot shove the accelerator as if he was taking it out on the car. His personality had changed recently, but she put it down to work. It wasn't easy managing a theatre. She herself was a bank manager, but they were two different things.

'Where is this place again?' she asked.

'Groucho's, George Street. It's new. I wanted us to try it out, my love.'

She felt sick at those words. Her lack of feelings for him had accelerated since she had told Sean. She sat and thought about that again and wondered not for the first time why she had shared her feelings with her ex-husband. But she knew why. There was no mistaking her feelings for him.

The job had got to her, and she knew that Sean was married to the job as well, but all she'd wanted was to be made to feel as if she was at least the most important thing in his life, and not the job.

Back then, she knew if she had voiced her opinion to him, sat him down and told him how she really felt, he would have done something stupid like jack it all in for her. He had spoken about going to live up north, just the two of them, finding a little house by a river where they could wake up to the sound of running water. Take hikes. Buy a dog and take him with them everywhere. It was a pipe dream, but it was nice to sit and talk about it every so often. She wanted to do it with him, but the timing had to be right, and at that time it wasn't.

That was why she had made up a story about cheating on him. She had fallen on the sword. She had watched the tears come into his eyes, had watched him break inside, and it had broken her heart to do it to him, but he had to stay with the job. She knew it would kill him to leave the job then. He was too young.

She hadn't contested anything, telling him he could have anything he wanted. She had even offered to walk away from the house they had bought together, but God bless him, he had insisted she get her half.

And then he had turned round and put in for a transfer to Fife. That had been a shock for her, and on more than one occasion she had felt an almost overwhelming sense of loss. That she should tell him the truth.

She had told him that she had been with other men – not many, but a couple of serious relationships. In fact, she had had no relationships. A few dates here and there, nothing serious, and she had never slept with any of them. The one man she loved more than anything in the world was on the other side of the Firth of Forth, and every night for the longest time she had cried herself to sleep wondering where her husband was.

And there were times like now when she felt like just calling him and telling him she had made a huge mistake, telling him that she had concocted a lie back then. But he was in a relationship now and she couldn't destroy that.

So here she was, driving to some fancy restaurant with Leon, a man she didn't love and barely liked anymore. If this was it, if he got down on one knee, she would tell him to stop being so bloody stupid. Yes, he would get angry and upset, but what was the worst that would happen? He would drive off and leave her stranded? She would call Sean at that point. Just as a friend, of course. He wouldn't see her stuck.

The little man drove the big car the same way he looked at life: *get out of my way*. On more than one occasion, Leon had given the finger to another driver; then when the man got out, he would wind the window up and lock the doors. That had been in his little foo-foo Italian roller-skate with the American name. Now he was in what must have felt like a Chieftain tank.

'Look at that fuck,' he said, pulling into the side of the road past the George Hotel. 'You'd think he's trying to park a bus.' He honked the horn for good measure and the elderly driver looked at the big car before deciding it would be best to move.

'Listen, Leon, I have a favour to ask.'

Leon turned the engine off and looked at her. 'Fire away.'

'Sean was asking if you could get him some tickets for the theatre. He'd like to take Chaz there for a night out.'

'Sure I can.'

'Terrific. He'll be pleased to hear that.'

'Come on then. Let's get inside. I have a surprise for you.'

He stepped out of the car – without the need for a parachute, Catherine noted – and then stood on the pavement, looking around. Instead of opening the door for her. If anything was going to help her make the decision to jump ship, this was it. That and the bloody lip he had been giving her.

She got out of the big car and saw he was looking at an old church.

'Make you feel like going back on a Sunday?' she asked.

'No. Just makes me feel like going to a church one day. I mean, for just one day. For a special occasion.'

'And what would that be?' she asked.

'This is the new restaurant I was telling you about,' he said, changing the subject and guiding her by the elbow.

She looked about and saw the sign proclaiming a new restaurant called *Groucho's*.

'It's just opened. You're going to love it. You'll remember this night for the rest of your life.'

So will you, she thought.

They approached the door, the cold wind blowing some snow around. Inside, they were greeted by a maître d', who showed them to the table that was reserved for them.

When they were seated, a waiter came over with a wine list, but Leon immediately ordered champagne.

'Leon, don't take this the wrong way, but this seems to be an expensive restaurant, and just the other week you were complaining about having no money. You even borrowed money from me for a new project you were working on.'

'I know. I want to go into business for myself. I want to open a restaurant, then one day we'll have a place like this. That's what the business loan is for.'

'Then I feel guilty for letting you bring me here, spending money you don't have.'

'It's just this one night, I promise. It's a special occasion.'

Catherine felt sick. Not having an appetite didn't even begin to cover how she felt. Then the champagne magically arrived, and when two glasses had been poured, Leon was ready to start the cabaret.

He reached into his pocket and brought out a little velvet box. He smiled across the table at her and was about to push his chair back when she reached over and put a hand over his.

'Don't, Leon.'

He looked at her, the smile dropping off his face. 'Why?'

'I don't want you to feel embarrassed. Tell me you weren't going to get on one knee and we can have dinner.'

'I was. Wasn't the chair being scraped back a heads-up?'

'That's exactly why I'm stopping you. I don't want you on your knee when I say no.'

'You would say no?' He looked like a five-year-old who'd just been told the tooth fairy had been arrested for fraud.

'I like you, Leon. I don't love you.' There, it was said. Out in the open. She felt relief and was about to add, *'Why can't we just have a nice dinner now?'* But she said nothing else.

'Oh, brilliant. You don't love me. Why have I been wasting my time with you these past few months? It wasn't because you were a good shag, because we haven't even slept together. Fuck me, I feel like the biggest clown in the world.'

The chair was shoved back again, so hard it tipped over. A waiter rushed over to pick it up for the little man.

'Fuck off. Leave it!' Leon snapped.

'Please sit down, Leon,' Catherine said. 'We can talk about this.'

'There's nothing to talk about. We're done. Finished. Don't call me again.'

'I can hardly do that anyway, can I?'

Leon had turned away, but now he stopped and turned back to face Catherine.

'What did you say?'

Catherine looked around at the other diners, who were getting a free show, like she and Leon were putting on a Festival Fringe play.

'You didn't give me your new number. I only saw it when you called me earlier.'

Leon laughed. 'Once a copper's wife, always a copper's wife, eh? Well, I'll have you know that I lost my phone and had to get a temporary one.' He shook his head. 'Always jumping to conclusions, eh?'

'I'm sorry, Leon.'

'You're just like the others. I thought you were different.'

Leon turned and walked out, not looking back. The waiter picked the chair back up and the manager approached Catherine.

'I'm assuming you won't be staying, ma'am?'

'Correct. I'll pay for the champagne.'

'Don't worry about it. It's on the house. Can I call somebody for you? Or a cab perhaps?' the manager said.

'I'll call somebody. If I could just wait in the lobby.'

'Of course. Allow me to escort you to the front.'

'The walk of shame. I can't believe he did that.'

She was already on the phone by the time they reached the front of the restaurant. 'Hello? Sean? You busy?'

TWENTY-SIX

Bob Long missed the days when he was a detective working as part of the MIT. Chasing down bad guys, taking the filth off the streets. Now he ran a guest house with his wife. He was grateful for the opportunity of course, but he missed the excitement most of all.

Today was no different, but he felt like he was operating on the outskirts. Something different from his normal day-to-day life.

The bungalow sat amongst a lot of other bungalows down in Craigentinny, but this one was different: its curtains were closed.

Bob knocked on the door. Three rapid, two slow, three rapid. Nothing that would confuse a Russian spy satellite, but it suited their needs at that time.

The door opened and there was nobody there.

'Nash, Bob,' said the person behind the door. Bob

nashed, stepping into the hallway and wiping the snow off his boots on a mat.

The door closed behind him and a young woman stood looking at him. He knew she was in her early thirties, but she could have passed for a fifteen-year-old. Detective Constable Sherrie Connor.

'It's been a while, Sherrie. You're looking good. Motherhood is obviously agreeing with you.'

'Thanks, Bob. You're looking good yourself. Retirement is obviously agreeing with *you*.'

'Apart from the boredom. I miss working.'

'Me too. That's why I'm going back to work as soon as I can. Brian is putting in as much overtime as possible. He's going for his inspector's exam later.'

Talk of the Devil, Bob thought, as Sherrie's husband poked his head round the living room door. 'Hi, Bob. Coffee?'

'Hey, Brian. No, thanks, son. I have a long drive home after this, and I don't want to be put on the sex offenders' list for having a pish on the bypass.'

'Give's a shout if either of you need anything. Craig's sleeping.'

'Thanks, love. We'll be in the office,' Sherrie said.

Brian gently closed the living room door.

'This way,' Sherrie said, leading Bob into one of the three bedrooms.

'I appreciate you seeing me,' he said, sitting down

on an office chair near a desk. Sherrie sat down on the other one in front of the computer. 'If Brian needs any advice, get him to give me a shout,' Bob said.

'No problem. I remember how you took me under your wing. You believed in me, Bob. I never forgot that. Plus, you stopped that drunken bastard from kicking me that night down by the docks. The doctor said if he had kicked me more, then I wouldn't have had a chance to have any children. You took the bastard down. If it wasn't for you, I wouldn't be here to have my husband and my wee boy.'

He saw tears in her eyes, despite the curtains being closed in this room as well.

'You would have done the same for me.'

'I told you to ask any time you needed my help on something.'

'And here I am, cap in hand. I don't know who else to turn to.'

Sherrie, who worked in the cyber crimes unit, smiled. 'Nobody better who knows their way round a keyboard,' she said. 'And if there's one person I'm happy to help, it's you, Bob. And I'm happy to say that I was able to accommodate you. I was able to get your friend's money back.'

'Not a penny more. That's what I stipulated. Just the exact amount of money that lassie stole from him.'

'Not a penny more. I bounced it around through so

many dummy accounts, nobody will be able to figure out where it went. And it landed in an old account that your friend has been adding to for years. Although technically, that account is only a day old, its history goes back years. It's all above board and nobody will question it. I also erased all of the deposits taken from his bank where he withdrew the money. There's no record of the money ever being in that account, only in the old one. So when he goes to take it out for a legitimate purpose, nobody will look twice at it.'

'Oh my God, you've gone above anything I expected,' Bob said. 'I just wanted to know if you could trace it.'

'That was easy. It seems they've been at it with other people too. One person we both know.'

'Who?' Bob looked puzzled.

'Catherine Bracken. Her money was given to somebody else, but it landed in the same account as Ed's had. Needless to say, I transferred it into Ed's. He can give it back to Catherine. Whoever took them to the cleaner's just had their arse felt. They won't know what hit them. They're in financial straits as it is, and this will hurt them.'

'Oh my God, Sherrie, I can't thank you enough.'

'You can thank me by coming along to Craig's christening. You and Mary.'

'Count us in. We'll be there.'

'Also, this never happened. You were never here.'

'Gotcha.'

They left the room and Brian poked his head round again. 'Good seeing you again, Bob.'

'You too, son. Good luck on the DI exam.'

'Thanks, sir.'

'Here, here, we'll have none of that. It's Bob.'

Detective Sergeant Brian Connor smiled. 'Catch you around, Bob.'

Sherrie saw him out, and as Bob drove away, he didn't think Sean Bracken would have any problem pulling some strings for the Connors.

TWENTY-SEVEN

Bracken sat in an office chair and wiped a hand over his face. He felt tired now. His old man was in an interview room giving a statement to Sullivan and young Doc. How the hell the old sod had got mixed up with Stella Mason was beyond him. Or Elizabeth as she was known.

'I was doing a little background search,' DS Izzie Khan said to him, turning from her computer. 'The Kelly family were very interesting.'

'In what way?'

'It seems like they were all daft. Two of the sisters ran away and have never been seen since. And we know all about Jerome, how he murdered Rita in Craigtoun. But there was the other one as well.'

'What other one? Oh, yeah. Ailsa mentioned that,' Bracken said, sitting up in the chair.

'The other brother. Robert Kelly. Seems he was always in trouble with the police, but nothing major. Always skirting the law. Whenever the police were called, Jerome would be there with him.'

'Where is this Robert now?'

'Well, well, would you believe it?' She told him.

'Get an address for him, please, Izzie.'

Then Bracken's phone rang.

'Hello? Sean? You busy?'

It was Catherine.

'I am. But what's up?'

'Listen, I'm sorry I didn't answer your call earlier. If you weren't busy, I would ask you to join me for a drink. I just dumped Leon in Groucho's and he didn't take it well.'

'Christ, Catherine, you have to stay away from him. He's dangerous.'

'He's not that bad. He's hardly the Hulk.'

'Which makes him even more dangerous. He left a murder scene earlier today. We have a "be on the look-out" issued for him. Was he in a red Jeep?'

'What? No, he was in a Range Rover.'

'Range Rover?'

'Yes. A big black thing with blacked-out windows.' There was a pause for a moment. *'Oh, Christ, he's back. He just pulled into the side of the road. I'm not going to*

be nice with him this time, Sean. I'm going to be blunt as hell. Let me call you back.'

'Catherine, no!' Bracken shouted into his phone, but she had hung up. He dialled her number, but it went to voicemail. 'I have to go,' he said. 'Catherine's with that little bastard.'

'Where?' Sullivan said, jumping to his feet.

'Groucho's.'

'East End, near the George Hotel,' Tam Gale said. 'The wife and I have been there. Pricey.'

'I need to get there.' Bracken grabbed his coat and wrestled it on.

'I'll drive,' Sullivan said.

'We're coming,' Tam Gale said. 'Doc, get your coat. Izzie, you too. We can take two cars.'

'Follow me. First of all, though, this is a photo of who we're looking for.' Bracken brought up Leon's photo on his phone, from the time they'd had a drink at Catherine's house. He showed it to them all.

'That's the guy who's on the Sunrise Productions website,' Izzie said. 'Only on there, he's known as Bernie Appleton. Jerome Kelly's mother's maiden name was Appleton.'

Catherine Bracken ended the call, put her phone into her bag and walked towards the Range Rover sitting at the kerb. She was going to let the little bastard have it.

She walked forward and the tinted windows stayed closed, then the passenger side one slid down a few inches and stopped.

'I'm sorry,' Leon Harris said. His eyes were wet like he'd been crying and his face looked pale.

'Oh, Leon. We weren't meant to be together forever.' She suddenly didn't have the heart to shout at him. He was like a little boy sitting there, waiting for punishment from his mother.

'I know that. Please get in. I'll drive you home.'

She wasn't going to. Sean had said Leon had left a murder scene. 'No, I can't, Leon.'

'In the back,' Leon said.

'What? I don't think so.'

Then there was somebody behind her, pressing something into her back. 'You heard the man. In the back. Or you can bleed out here in the snow.'

She heard the clunk of the doors being unlocked and then the back door was opened and she got in.

'Move to the other side, behind Jerome,' the man behind her instructed.

'Who?'

Then she was roughly pushed and she fell into the big car. She moved over to the seat behind the man she knew as Leon but now was finding out she didn't know at all.

The other man climbed in. There were no lights on in the car but still she recognised him.

'No. It can't be.'

The car took off.

TWENTY-EIGHT

The two cars pulled into the yard and Bracken saw
there were no lights on in the Portakabin. There had
been no sign of Catherine up at the restaurant and the
manager had told them she had got into a black Range
Rover.

'Christ, if they're not here, then where the hell are
they?' Sullivan had said. Bracken could think of only
one other place.

Now they were down in Leith.

'Over there,' Bracken said, seeing that the door on
the right-hand side of the roller door was open and
light was spilling out.

He looked in the mirror and saw the other car pull
in behind them. He got out and instructed the others to
follow.

'He's dangerous,' Bracken told them. 'Don't take

any chances, but let's not go in there like bulls in a china shop.'

He saw the police vans pull into the side of the road outside. The Leith contingent. He was pleased to see them bail out without slamming the doors. When they were grouped, Bracken spoke to them.

'Let us go in first and scout the place out. If we need you, we'll shout.'

'Yes, sir,' the sergeant said.

Bracken walked forward with Sullivan by his side, and Tam Gale, Izzie and Doc behind them. Bracken approached the red door and saw all the lights were on in the big warehouse. There was some camera equipment sitting over to one side, but a pile of boxes hid the view of the rest of the interior. He began to step round them.

'You fucking did this!' a voice screamed.

'Jerome Kelly?' Sullivan whispered to Bracken.

'Has to be,' Bracken answered, walking past the rest of the pile into the main part of the warehouse. It couldn't be described as football-stadium sized, but it was big enough.

It wasn't Jerome Kelly who was shouting. It was his brother, Robert. Or, as he was better known, Desmond Rough.

'You just had to have a little side business going with that stupid bitch Stella, didn't you? Screwing people like that old man. And this cow! This...fucking whore that you were sleeping with.'

'I thought she would marry me. That's why I wanted her money. When she began making it clear that she wasn't interested, I told Stella to go and screw her father-in-law for everything the old man has. So Stella became Elizabeth and took his money.'

Bracken had heard enough. He could just make out the two men arguing, but he couldn't see Catherine for more piles of boxes. Then, as he got closer, he could see her sitting on a chair, her hands tied to it.

'How should I address you?' Bracken said. 'Robert or Desmond?'

'Don't you come any closer!' Rough said to Bracken. 'I'll put this bag over her head.'

'Just like the others? Just like Rita, thirty years ago? Where you left Jerome to take the blame?' Bracken nodded to the man he knew as Leon Harris. 'We know all about it. Peter Solomon, Rita's father, spoke to Jerome in the hospital when he was first incarcerated.'

Rough looked at Jerome Kelly. 'You did what?'

'You left me with Rita. She was my friend, but you and Audrey killed her.'

'She was pregnant! I couldn't let her drag me down. And Audrey was just there. She didn't touch Rita.'

'Your moods drove our sisters to run away. I was

left with you until Rita came into my life. But you had to take her away too.'

'I gave you a new life as Bernie Appleton, didn't I? You were an executive. We could have made a go of this.'

Bracken stepped closer. 'Why did you kill Claire?' he said to Rough.

'Because of that stupid podcast stuff. Audrey called me and told me her father was dying. That she'd had enough of this and wanted to put it behind her, knowing who had killed her sister that day. She told her daughter about me, and she said that Stewie Anderson knew as well. So they all had to go. I should have taken care of Audrey as well as Rita all those years ago. Never mind. Thirty years in the making. I could make a good documentary about this.'

'From prison,' Jimmy Sullivan said.

'I'll still be famous.'

'Do you remember me, Jerome?' Bracken said. 'In the supermarket, twenty years ago. You were fighting with that man.'

'I don't remember you. I remember fighting him. I knew Diane. I was just looking at the baby. Her husband made me angry.'

'I wanted them to put Jerome in Carstairs,' Rough said, 'so I killed Diane. Made it look like Rita's murder. And still they let him out. The system is well fucked.'

'And then Claire was going to spill the beans and ruin everything you'd worked for all these years.'

'Yes. But I could still do it, with these morons out the way.'

'Don't you think Jerome there would have told us about you killing Catherine? He's in love with her.'

'He was going to die too. He would have hanged himself from the rafters. Case closed. But this isn't over until the fat lady sings. Although she's not fat.'

Rough ran at Catherine with the heavy-gauge plastic bag, and Bracken started running, but he could see he wouldn't make it.

Then Leon Harris – or Bernie Appleton or Jerome Kelly – stepped forward. Bracken didn't know what personality had emerged, but whoever it was, the knife in his pocket came out and caught Desmond Rough in the throat. Blood spurted into the air and Rough fell to his knees.

Leon Harris turned to Catherine. 'I love you. I can't go back there. I'm sorry for what I did.' Then he stuck the knife in the carotid in his neck and his blood joined his brother's.

Catherine screamed as blood covered her just before Bracken got there.

Then all hell broke loose as the uniforms rushed in.

Bracken looked down at the men. Both of them were dead.

TWENTY-NINE

They sat in the dining room of the guest house, a drink in front of them. Chaz sat beside Catherine and they were busy catching up.

'All the money's back in my account,' Ed Bracken said. 'God knows how.'

Bob looked away.

'Catherine got her money back too,' Bracken said in a low voice. 'I hope you learned a bloody lesson from this. Keep it in your Y-fronts from now on.'

'Enough of that bloody talk.'

'You with a teenage stepson. I can just see it now.'

'I would have skelped his bloody arse. I learned a lesson alright: spare the rod and spoil the child.'

Bob clinked a glass with a spoon. 'Ladies and gentlemen, join me in raising a glass to Catherine. Safe and sound.'

'To Catherine,' they chanted.

They tucked into their dinner and Bracken looked across at Chaz and Catherine, both of them thick as thieves. He knew then he was going to have to make a decision about the direction his life was going in.

He thought he knew the answer.

AUTHOR'S NOTE

The incident in Chapter 1 really did happen. To me. It was the inspiration for this novel. A man grabbed my youngest daughter, who was a few months old at the time, and of course I told him to stop. He took exception to this and assaulted me. I'm six foot two and this guy was bigger than me (not like in the book, with Jerome Kelly being small), and he rammed me into the shelves. Like most dads, instinct kicked in and just the thought of him touching my baby enraged me. He tried to clap his hands on my ears, but I pulled my head back, and yes, I really did ram him onto the juice cartons. He was strong and taunted me.

Then, before I knew what was happening, I got hauled off him by four men, and the manager was raging. He told me the police were on the way and I would be arrested. Until I told him that the guy had touched my baby and had assaulted me. 'Check your CCTV cameras,' I told him, 'I was defending myself.' Then he had that *'oh, shit'* look on his face, and all hell broke loose.

There was chaos as they looked for him. The guy had got up and run off, and a security team caught him trying to get on a bus. A police officer – not there to arrest me – told me that the procurator fiscal would do nothing as this guy was known to the police and had just been released from Gogarburn psychiatric hospital into the care of the community. I was not happy about that at all. He was clearly dangerous. If I hadn't fought the way I had, he might have got the better of me and God knows what he would have done.

Months later, I was on a bus and I saw him talking to a little girl who was with her mother. I won't tell you what I wanted to do to him.

So that was how this story was born. It's been 22 years in the making.

That just leaves me to thank some people.

Ruth, as always, for her help. The other John Carson. Thanks to Jim Brown and especially to Jacqueline Beard. To my editor, Charlie Wilson, a huge thank you. Thank you to my wife, who entertains the dogs when they're not with me in the office, which they are most days. She's the most valued member of Team Carson.

Lastly, thank you to my readers. You are all special to me. And if I could please ask you to consider leaving a review or a rating, that would be fantastic. I appreciate each and every one.

One more thing before I go - "DSup Gladstone had a face like a Crowded House album cover" – Woodface, in case you were wondering. Check it out, it's a great album.

Stay safe, my friends.

John Carson
New York
December 2021

Made in the USA
Las Vegas, NV
28 December 2021

39742857R00135